Show time!

Amanda looked hurriedly at Joe, shirt untucked, but chest untouched, and she was still all ironed and buttoned. "We don't look like we've been *doing* anything!" she wailed. The doorbell rang again. "This is supposed to look torrid. Avery has to think he doesn't stand a chance."

Joe lowered his voice. "This was your idea. What are we supposed to do? Get a little down and dirty on the carpet and just let Avery walk right in?"

The doorbell rang for a third time.

"I'm coming," Joe yelled, still standing several feet away from Amanda, looking completely untorrid.

"Look, if this were a *real* date, what would Avery expect to find?" She wanted to know exactly what was the current fashion for being found in flagrante delicto.

Joe's smile was slow, but smoky. "Babe, if this were for real, you'd be lucky to have your socks."

Wow.

Dear Reader,

I love New York; I have always loved New York. However, there seems to be a whole side to the city and the people that gets forgotten in all the glamour and glitz. And that was my inspiration for Joe, all surly exterior and tough-guy looks, but who can still see great things in an ordinary world.

I started writing this story before September 11 of last year, and finished it afterward. Joe changed as I started telling his tale. He wasn't as carefree, nor was he as prone to crack jokes; he even got a little cranky. Yet in his character I found something special and strong, something warm and vibrant, willing to fight against all odds.

That something was the spirit of the city. This one's for you.

Kathleen O'Reilly

Books by Kathleen O'Reilly

HARLEQUIN DUETS
66—A CHRISTMAS CAROL

JUST KISS ME
Kathleen O'Reilly

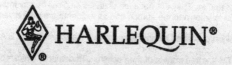

HARLEQUIN®

TORONTO • NEW YORK • LONDON
AMSTERDAM • PARIS • SYDNEY • HAMBURG
STOCKHOLM • ATHENS • TOKYO • MILAN • MADRID
PRAGUE • WARSAW • BUDAPEST • AUCKLAND

There are some people who helped me to understand
and appreciate the job that airline mechanics perform
each and every day. Mike "Buzz" Meyer, Corey Ford
and all the other folks on CompuServ who volunteered
to help. There are a lot of heroes in the world, and
sometimes we just overlook them. Not in this book.

ISBN 0-373-25989-1

JUST KISS ME

Visit us at www.eHarlequin.com

Printed in U.S.A.

1

BACK ME UP ON THIS, PLEASE!

Joe Barrington refocused on the tiny letters that were precisely inked into the cocktail napkin, working to scramble the letters into a happier meaning.

Well, she'd actually done it. After twenty-one years of fighting her own battle in futility, she had decided to ask for his help. He should tell her no.

His mouth even formed the words, but when Joe looked up and stared into the fathomless blue eyes of Amanda Sedgewick, he knew he was as perfectly cooked as the Manhattan restaurant's world famous pâté de foie gras.

Damn. Well, he wouldn't go down without a fight.

"No," he mouthed the words. He shook his head, just in case she missed what he was saying.

"Please." Amanda mouthed back him, shooting one of those helpless female looks that under different circumstances might have worked wonders on him.

However, he'd never been one of those knights who rode around saving damsels in distress. Nope. Not even close. There were chinks in his armor. Big chinks. Huge chinks.

With a heavy sigh, he stared across the pristine tablecloth at the proud visage of Dr. Avery Barrington, III, his big brother, who was currently studying the wine list like it was the *Wall Street Journal*. And there sat Joe's biggest chink.

Avery. The whole world revolved around Avery.

Before Avery had reached the advanced age of eight, he had mapped out his entire future. Mainly because in elementary school, life really sucked for guys named Avery. First, he was going to become a doctor in order to get rich just to spite those bullies who picked on the Averys of the world. And second, to further their torment, he was equally determined to marry the most beautiful girl at Neil Armstrong Elementary, who just happened to be—Amanda.

It was a simple plan, and Joe applauded his brother's single-minded pursuit of his goals. He'd achieved them all. Avery was a wealthy plastic surgeon, the bullies from grade school were gas attendants with beer bellies, he graduated at the top of his class from Columbia, he drove a German car, but for Avery there was still one big fly stuck in the soup.

Amanda.

The last time Joe had seen her was Avery's high school graduation. Tonight he had been surprised to see she had developed a maturity that had been missing before. She was still gorgeous, but now there was a confidence in the way she held herself and the way she talked. Just like Avery.

Which brought Joe right back to the plea for help

on the cocktail napkin. Well, whatever she wanted him to back her up on, it wasn't going to happen. Joe firmly believed that Avery's love life, sterile and lifeless as it was, was none of his business.

"Not my problem." Joe stated his case categorically, meeting her eyes so there was no misunderstanding. For twenty-one years he had stayed out of the whole thing, listening to Avery rhapsodize about Amanda's porcelainlike features, and thinking yeah, she was okay if you liked cool blondes with impeccable fashion sense.

But Joe liked his women with fire in their blood and sin in their eyes. He smiled, fondly reminiscing about his last date. Sometimes it was hard to believe he and Avery shared the same genes. Maybe they didn't. It would explain a lot. Why Joe hadn't got into St. Alban's preparatory school, when Avery had. Why Avery wanted to make people well, and Joe just wanted to be around planes.

The wine steward came to the table and wisely, Joe and Amanda let Avery make the selection. Amanda shot Joe another meaningful look. *"Please,"* she mouthed again. Then she lifted her palms, a suffering angel. Right.

Avery placed the order, and then turned back to Joe. "What were you saying?"

"I was telling Amanda that, no, I'm not going to do anything with her cocktail napkin. Thanks very much for offering." He passed the white paper back to her, wondering why she had even agreed to go

out to dinner with Avery in the first place and even
more mysteriously, why she had wanted Joe to come
along.

Amanda smiled politely, took the napkin in her
perfectly manicured hands and sat her water glass
down top of it. Amanda never gave anything away.
She was the perfect complement for his brother, the
liberal sophisticate.

Everything except that mouth.

In a face composed of high cheekbones and un-
blinking eyes, her mouth was wild and wicked. Full,
red lips that curled up slightly at the corners, as if she
had a secret and you knew that no matter how you
tried, you'd never discover it.

Joe knew Amanda had secrets, that there was a
hidden piece of her that she never showed, and he
didn't know whether it was the poised exterior or
the promise of that mouth that inspired his brother.

But that was none of his business.

Finally, she raised one eyebrow, a challenge. Then
she turned to Avery, and brushed her hair back on
her shoulders. Very smooth. Of course, Amanda was
a lawyer, and she knew all the moves. "It's not going
to work," she said.

Huh?

Amanda picked up her glass of wine and watched
Joe, her mouth curving ever so slightly. He shifted,
not liking that provocative smile blasting in his direction. She turned to Avery. "It's time I was honest
with you."

About time. And that sounded like his cue to leave. Joe stood. "Excuse me. I'm sure you two need a little privacy. I'll just take a train home."

"No!" All traces of steel vanished from her voice, her blue eyes soft and pleading. Avery heaved a theatrical sigh.

Surely she didn't expect Joe to stick around while she had *The Talk* with his brother? Not that Joe thought it would do a bit of good. Avery would never give up. He could bulldoze the entire third world if he put his mind to it, and Joe gave Amanda high marks for managing to escape un-dozed. So far.

"I think we need to tell your brother this together."

We? There it was again. The whispered tone, that intimate look. Like lovers. A guy could get really used to that look.

And then it all clicked. Joe. Amanda. Lovers.

Holy Cow.

"Uh, no, I don't think so," he answered, every cell in his body flashing red-alert. There were some cells that were flashing more enthusiastically than others, and Joe shifted uncomfortably. He tried for a paternally disapproving voice. "You should have talked to me before you decided to bring this up."

And still she stared at him, and he almost forgot his good intentions. He almost forgot Avery. Which was a hard thing to do.

Thankfully, the wine steward came, and placed the bottle of wine on the table, waiting for Avery's approval. Then the ritual began. Avery sniffed, whirled, sipped and finally nodded. The steward poured everyone a glass and then departed in silence.

"What did you want to tell me, Amanda?" Avery asked.

Amanda shot Joe one last pleading look. He almost caved. He'd pretty well figured it out. Joe and Amanda, pretend lovers. Absolutely without question, the most harebrained scheme she'd ever had to get rid of Avery. Of course, Amanda didn't do harebrained well, and Avery wasn't very cooperative as a dumpee.

"Avery, I'm in love with Joe."

Her harebrained skills were improving by the minute.

It was a valiant struggle not to spew cabernet all over the pristine, white tablecloth, but he managed. He'd thought she was proposing an affair, but no, this was Amanda. Of course the lawyer would want it all. She'd say she was in love. With Joe.

Was she nuts?

He took another hasty swallow of wine. He had *really* underestimated her this time. Who knew that beneath that cool exterior lurked Lucille Ball? No foul though, because, of course, Avery would never believe it.

Feeling rather confident of his prediction, Joe turned to Avery. Three. Two. One.

"Joe?" Avery spluttered, predictable as always. "You can't be serious! He's an *airline mechanic*."

And so it goes. Joe sighed and began to butter his bread. "Thanks, Ave. Love you too, bro."

But Amanda wasn't done yet and if Avery wasn't blood-kin, Joe would have felt sorry for her. "I *am* serious, Avery. It's something I've been fighting for a long time." She turned to Joe, her wicked mouth trembling. "Something *we've* been fighting for a long time. I can't let you ruin this for me, Avery. I won't let you ruin my one chance at happiness."

Avery's face was all screwed up and confused, not a pretty sight. "But why Joe?"

Enjoying himself now, and feeling quite safe, Joe took a bite. He couldn't wait to hear the answer to this one.

She pushed at her perfectly coiffed hair as if a strand had fallen in her eyes, which of course, it hadn't. "Because I'm tired of being restrained and constricted and having to iron my clothes." She took a deep breath, the neckline of her white linen dress rising discreetly. "I want to stop worrying about what I say, and who I have to meet and whether my nails are done."

Oh, she was good. If not for the plea for help on her napkin, he might have believed her. He wasn't going to back her up on this tale, though. Avery might be pompous and stubborn and a little bit weird, but he was his brother. And if Joe had been named Avery, he might have turned out just like him.

"I don't understand the connection between your nails and Joe." Avery frowned and rubbed a finger against his brow.

"There isn't one. There doesn't always have to be a reason or an explanation. Sometimes things just are. Joe doesn't worry about having to be something, he's just happy being."

Avery assumed his doctor face, which looked so much like their father's. "Sounds damned irresponsible to me."

It sounded pretty irresponsible to Joe, too, but he was impressed that Amanda had enough depth to figure that part of him out.

"It's not irresponsible, it's serenity," she said.

He almost laughed out loud at that. Serenity? Sounded more like New Age crap. He wondered if he should interrupt now and put an end to the whole nonsense. He wouldn't have his brother hurt. Though it pricked at him that Avery acted more appalled than spurned. Just for that, Joe leaned back and folded his arms across his chest.

He'd stop it in a minute.

Avery smoothed out his napkin, then began folding it into precise triangles. "Serenity? You're spouting that mystic mumbo jumbo, next you'll be telling me you've decided to go off on some mission to find yourself. Amanda, you're a beautiful woman. Be happy with who you are."

"Avery, you're a wonderful man, and I do love you in a special way, but I will never love you like that."

"Well, of course you will. In time you'll see sense." Avery rummaged through his pocket for the package of stomach medicine he carried with him. He swallowed two white tables and turned on Joe, obviously deciding that Joe was somehow responsible for this. "You've seduced her, haven't you? I should call you out." Always the dramatic one—he got that from their mother—Avery stood and slapped his napkin on the table.

"Now, Avery, sit down. There's no need to make a scene." Amanda put a hand to his arm.

Magic words to Avery who despised making a scene. He obediently sat.

"Nothing has ever happened between the two of us." She cast a calming smile in Joe's direction. "Joe is much too honorable to do anything while you are so, um, fixated."

Avery shot a questioning glance in Joe's direction, and Joe nodded. *Damn straight.*

Amanda cleared her throat and squared her shoulders and pierced Avery with a steely gaze. "However, I think it's time that you stepped aside, and let me and your brother be happy."

Joe watched her, silently applauding her acting skills. It was easy to imagine her in the courtroom. *"And for his considerable pain and suffering, my client deserves nothing less than ten million dollars...."*

However, Avery, who never got picked for juries, still wasn't buying it. He turned to Joe, using his doctor face again. "Is this true?"

Joe looked from his brother, who looked just a little smug, to Amanda, who looked just a little desperate. It was a tough choice and his conscience even tweaked him a bit. Avery's dedication to Amanda wasn't exactly fair to her, but Joe stood with his brother. Now and always. He might be irresponsible, but he was loyal to a fault. "Absolutely not. She's lying. Don't believe a word of it."

Amanda twisted the spoon between her fingers, that one little move giving her away. She was ticked.

"Avery, can I talk to Joe alone please? He didn't want to do this tonight." She shot Avery a pleading look. "Just a few minutes."

Avery frowned, looking displeased with the idea, but he was too polite to stay, so he stood, and stuck his hands in his tweed jacket. Looking as dignified as always, he scanned the dining room. "Well, it looks like Mrs. Hoyton-Spenser is awaiting her dinner companion. I suppose I should go say hello."

AMANDA STUDIED her nails to buy precious time, and wondered if she shouldn't have talked to Joe in advance. Of course he would have said no, which was why she had taken the coward's way out and waited until he couldn't say no. It was such a brilliant plan, though and she told him so.

"It's brilliant. Why don't you admit it?"

"You're insane! What happened to telling him you're not interested?"

Joe and Avery didn't look a thing alike. Joe was dark. Dark wavy hair, tanned skin. Avery was golden. Fair hair and a determined gleam in his eyes. The blue eyes were similar though. Except Avery's were placid and calm, like a cool, mountain lake. Joe's eyes were exotic and dangerous, like the waters of the Caribbean.

"Do you know how many times I've told him that? You're his brother, you know how he is. I can't divert him."

Joe pulled at his tie and leaned forward, elbows on the table. "But this is ridiculous! Every other female in America knows how to dump a guy."

"Joe, I've been dumping your brother for," she looked at her watch, "twenty-one years. I like him. He's sweet in a stuffy kinda of way. I've returned his gifts, made up excuses, gone out with other guys. Heavens, this is the first date I've been out on with him, and I made him bring you."

"It's the second. You went to the junior varsity football game with him at St. Albans."

When did his memory get to be so good? "How did you know?"

"Avery talked about it for weeks. That night he was the envy of every guy who had ever beat him up. You always were doing nice things for him."

"He didn't deserve to be bullied like that."

"No." Joe stared off at his brother.

Amanda adjusted her forks. They were getting sidetracked. Both of them cared for Avery. "My point being, you're the only way I know of to get him to move on with his life."

Joe looked at her and raised his brows. "Get another guy."

There's the rub. Oh, she'd tried, but every date she'd ever been on could be summed up in one word: boring. Honestly, she was afraid *she* was boring. She didn't want boring. She wanted Coney Island, with someone to teach her how to really live. She wanted a man who ate his jalapeños whole. And she'd found him. "Joe, I've tried dating other men. Nothing changed."

Joe sighed. "Get married, then. I bet he'd get the message."

"I'm not getting married just to get rid of Avery." Marriage? She wasn't ready to get married. Heck, she didn't even want commitment. No, she wanted an affair, with a capital *A*. And she'd found just the guy. The perfect guy for a no-strings-attached, screaming good time. And the best part? Finally, Avery would leave her alone. Just thinking about an affair with Joe made her smile. They'd spend Sunday mornings lazing in bed, reading the paper, making love. She closed her eyes, feeling tiny tremors dance across her skin.

That wouldn't do; she needed to stay focused. She opened her eyes and folded her hands in her lap. "Let me explain. What if we pretend to be passionately in love for say, two or three months? That's all. I have tons of friends that I think would be perfect for him. I'll fix him up, he'll move on and then I'll be free."

He didn't look convinced; really more skeptical than anything. "Why do you think he'll move on?"

Why were men dense at the most inopportune times? "Joe, for you, he would step aside. It's the noble thing to do. And Avery is nothing if not noble."

Joe shook his head mutinously, as stubborn as Avery at times. "He'll never forgive me."

"In a few years, he'll thank you." She was completely wrong for Avery; they'd bore each other to tears. "Imagine this. We're on a double date. I have a veritable cornucopia of sorority sisters who would enjoy the company of a prominent plastic surgeon. We'll go to dinner and Avery acts rather dejected. She asks what's wrong. He tells her he's been betrayed by his brother and that his one true love is no longer true. He would love it!"

Joe raised his dark brows. Oh, he had such a great face. All lines and angles and a nose that he'd broken not once but twice. How could a woman not lust after a guy who'd actually broken his nose?

There she was, getting herself distracted again. She got back to the subject at hand. "Okay, so maybe I'm overstating things a bit, but you must admit, it has a certain Shakespearian flair that Avery would enjoy wallowing in for a while."

"I don't know." At last, progress. He was beginning to waver.

"Joe, I'm not going to break down after twenty-one years and suddenly fall in love with him. It's time for everyone to stop pretending that my future is preordained as Mrs. Avery Barrington." She stared at her hands, nine perfectly polished fingernails and one that was short and ragged. She allowed herself one nail, but never more.

"Avery would never believe this. We have nothing in common. Hell, I haven't seen you in ten years before tonight."

"Avery doesn't know that and besides, we spent our formative years together. That counts for something."

"Going to the same church for ten years does not count as the basis for a relationship."

"Opposites attract."

"You're not my type. Avery *does* know that."

Ah, he'd overcome the emotional issues and was now moving to the logical. She had prepared her arguments for both.

"As it stands now, you're right. But I think it's time to live a little. Let my hair down, metaphorically speaking, of course."

He drummed his fingers on the table and she studied his rough and callused hands, imagining what it would be like to feel their touch. The tremors began again. Joe was the kind of guy who inspired tremors, and fantasies. Wild, wanton fantasies that involved motorcycles and possibly leather.

Well, today she was going after her fantasy. "Joe, in the long run, this is the best thing for him. This can't be healthy. He should be married, populating the world with little Averies that he can train in his image. I'm not the woman for him."

"I don't know. I think you both are perfect for each other."

That's what everyone else said, too. Frankly, she'd grown tired of it. "Then you don't know me."

"Guess not." He cocked his head, studying her, and she wished he could see more inside her than just the facade. "Not going to do it, Amanda. I won't hurt Avery."

"Joe, you're doing him more harm letting him waste his prime dating years stuck on me."

"It's wrong."

"Joe, Avery is thirty. How many dates has he been on?"

Joe thought for a minute. "A handful, I think."

"How many girlfriends?"

"Besides you?"

She dug her nails into her palms wanting to scream. "I don't count!" Still, a few people stared.

"None."

She lowered her voice. "Joe, Avery is probably still a virgin."

Joe laughed. "Uh, no. There was this..." He cut himself off and cleared his throat. "But that was a long time ago and it's none of my business." He took a sip of wine. "I'm not going to do it. There's got to be a better way."

There was no other way. "Fine. Name it. You give me some idea of how I can get your brother to move on with his life, and I'll forget all about the idea. One. Just one little thing I can do."

Joe sipped his wine, stared at Avery, shaking hands across the room, and sighed in defeat. "Pretend dating, huh?"

Finally. "More than dating. He's got to be convinced it's real, passionate, something that will make him think he doesn't stand a chance. A torrid affair." She loved the way the words sounded, coming out of her mouth.

He turned pale. "Torrid?"

She nodded. "Torrid."

Awareness flared in his blue eyes and all that exotic fire shot in her direction. She struggled to breath. He smiled. "Princess, I don't think you can do torrid."

"Is that a wager?" she managed.

As quickly as it came, the fire was gone. He was back to looking at her like everyone did. Avery's girl. "You think this plan of yours will really work?"

"I'm willing to bet on it, aren't I?" She held out her hand across the table, waiting. "Are you in?"

He stared for a moment, and her heart began to pound. He had never touched her, in twenty-one years, never once. She had dreamed, imagined, fantasized and now she was going to discover how his skin felt against her own. He wrapped one rough, calloused palm over her silky smooth hand and the tremors started in earnest.

"I'm not going to hurt my brother," he said, his voice sounding faraway because he was still touching her, and her entire nervous system was threatening to explode.

She swallowed. "I don't want to hurt him either, but I'm not about to marry him just because I think he's a nice guy."

He stayed silent for a moment, then dropped her hand. "I'm not going to rub his nose in this."

Under the table, where he couldn't see, her fingers traced the spot where Joe had touched her. "Rub his nose in it? You saw him. He doesn't even believe it. Yet."

"So, what do we do?"

"Well," she pretended to think about it for a moment. "We go out on a few dates. Maybe he could catch me over at your apartment a few times... What does Avery usually know about the women you—date?"

Joe smiled, satisfied and smug, obviously recalling past—dates. Amanda wanted to smack him. Not jealous, not jealous, not jealous.

Thankfully, she saw Avery heading back, arrogant and harmless. Why couldn't Avery be a jerk? It would make things so much easier. Instead, he was like a full-grown puppy dog. She sighed. "Look,

Avery's coming back. Tonight we'll ease into this thing and just see what happens. Maybe it'll be easier than you think." Amanda doubted it, but miracles could happen.

Joe shook his head. "If he gets extra weird, I'm bailing, Amanda. I can't see how this can be a good thing."

At last. Acceptance. "Okay, okay. Just let me do the talking."

He spread his hands wide. "You're the shyster."

Oh, fudge, this was going to be harder than she thought. "Cut the cracks. Remember we're supposed to be deeply in lust."

Joe just laughed; obviously thinking such an idea was ludicrous. *Just you wait, Joe, just you wait.*

WHEN AVERY RETURNED, he looked calm as ever. Which could only be a good thing, Joe thought. Somebody needed to be calm. Joe sure as hell wasn't. Insane was the actual word that flashed in Joe's mind.

With surgical precision, Avery placed his napkin in his lap; a graceful gesture that was obviously for their benefit. First Avery looked at Amanda and then back to Joe. "Well?"

Amanda began first. "As I said..."

Avery held up his hand. "No. I want to hear what Joe has to say."

Damn. Joe had never been prepared at school, that's why he'd been exiled into public education, and he certainly couldn't win at a debate with his brother. He kept it simple. "She's right."

Avery leaned forward and Joe got that awful spider-in-the-web feeling. "Joe, are you really in love with Amanda, or are you just after a temporary diversion that is several plateaus above your normal standards?"

What was he supposed to say? Avery was his brother. He stalled, not quite ready to commit himself yet. "Avery, if I *were* in love with Amanda, what would you do?"

Avery took a sip of water. "And she was in love with you?"

Joe nodded.

Avery stroked his chin. "If the two of you were truly in love, I couldn't interfere."

Amanda shot Joe her female "told-you-so" look. "However," Avery continued, "I fully expect this little walk on the wild side to run its course after a short time. A very short time."

Avery lifted his glass and swirled the wine, but Joe wasn't fooled. This was serious to Avery. "Are you in love with her, Joe?"

He didn't like lying to his brother; there were better ways of ducking the truth, but maybe Amanda had it right after all. Joe clinked Avery's glass with his own and nodded.

Instead of dejection, Avery's smile was full of that same smug confidence that had got him accepted at

St. Albans, a scholarship to Columbia. "Then may the best man win."

Joe closed his eyes and sunk into his seat. *No way.* Why hadn't he seen this coming? He was not going to enter into some hellish competition with his brother. When it came to Avery, Joe always lost.

Amanda poked him with her fork under the table and he shot her a dirty look. He didn't deserve that.

But he'd gotten himself in too far. She'd sucked him right into her little pact with the devil, and so he just smiled weakly. "Yeah."

This was such a bad idea.

2

IT HAD ONLY BEEN ONE DAY. Amanda traced the white petals of the orchid with her finger. Orchids of all things. She glanced about her office, for the first time hating the stark white modern décor that she herself had picked out two years ago. White art deco chairs, an uncluttered glass desk and unadorned soft white walls. In New York City, everything was a fashionable black or a muted gray, and she had always liked white. It was clean, pure and now unfortunately, her office was more like a hospital. Cold. Like the orchids.

Mentally she gathered her courage, lifted the receiver and dialed Avery's pager. She followed the computerized instructions, entered her phone number and made notes on how she would redecorate her office.

A few minutes later, Grace, the latest temp, walked in, wearing her new Statue of Liberty sunglasses. Secretarial temps were usually ghosts that flitted around the office, not wanting to be noticed at all. Grace was different. She was a perpetual tourist trapped in the body of a temporary secretary—proof that God had a sense of humor. "Dr. Barrington for you, Amanda." She lifted her shades. "Should I make an excuse?"

"No, thanks, Grace."

"Whatever you say, boss." Grace left Amanda alone with the blinking phone line.

Amanda stared at the flashing light and then picked up the phone. Saying "no" to Avery had never come easy to her; perhaps secretly he had sensed that. Whatever the reason, Amanda still hated discussing it. One day. Hopefully soon.

"Avery?"

"Yes? You paged?"

"Why did you send me orchids?"

"Did Joe send you orchids as well?"

Amanda sighed heavily into the mouthpiece, making sure he heard it. "No."

"Well, there. Your beauty calls for a rarer flower. Something long and delicate. Wasn't it Robert Frost who said, 'Sometimes I wander out of beaten ways, half looking for the orchid Calypso.'"

"Avery, that's very pretty, but I told you, I love Joe." Saying the words gave her a wicked thrill. Okay, it was lust, not love. But the lust was beginning to feel rather overpowering.

As usual, Avery ignored her. "I've been offered two tickets to *The Producers* for tonight."

"I've already got a date."

"With Joe?"

"Yes."

"Where's he taking you? I hope someplace that

epitomizes a marvelous dining adventure. Have you tried that new French bistro on the Upper East Side? Très Appétissant."

"We're staying in tonight." She maintained a meaningful silence, hoping he'd think that she and Joe would be having wild, passionate sex. She hoped that they *would* be having wild, passionate sex. Probably not yet, though. It was too soon. But when?

Avery coughed.

Enough about sex. "We're renting a movie. Popcorn. Butter."

"How *bourgeois*. I'm sure if Joe could afford better, he'd take you there."

"Don't be a snob, Avery. Everyone is an adult here."

"I'm sorry, Amanda. I've never been a graceful loser. Not that I think the war is over, not by any stretch of the imagination. I have not yet begun to fight."

That's what she was afraid of. "Avery?"

"Yes?"

"I have a deposition to go to. I'll talk to you later. No more flowers, hmmm?"

She hung up before he could reply and immediately dialed the airport. "Joe Barrington, please."

In the background, she heard the thunder of the planes, pounding tools and voices yelling, with a particular New York flavor. La Guardia. Laughing, she took notes, learning a few new fun words. Finally, Joe picked up. "Barrington."

"Joe? It's Amanda."

"What's up?"

"I told Avery we were watching a movie tonight."

"Yeah? What's that got to do with me?"

She gritted her teeth. "I think we need to watch a movie at your apartment."

"No offense, Amanda, but I've got a date tonight."

A date? "You're still dating?"

"Yeah."

"Is this serious?" Nervously, she twisted the barrel of her ballpoint pen back and forth.

"Define serious."

"How long have you been seeing this person?"

"I met her two nights ago."

"Joe! What do you think your brother will do when he finds out? He'll think you're cheating on me!"

"He won't know."

"Joe!" She picked up her pen, jotted a few more choice words on her notepad and then crossed them out again. "You want this to work, right?"

A power-drill whirred in the background. "It's not going to work."

"It won't work unless you have a positive attitude and a celibate existence."

"You didn't tell me this was a requirement last night."

She didn't reply.

"You're killing me, here."

"Joe, doing without sex will not kill you."

"But it can make a man awfully grumpy." Thankfully, he acquiesced soon enough. "All right. I suppose Monique will understand."

Monique? Trust Joe to pick up girls named Monique. "For the duration, Joe. It's going to take several months for this to work."

"Several months? Are you serious?" A pause and then his voice dropped. "Look, I can keep my private life private. Avery will never know."

"Joe."

"I'm not a monk. I'm not even a monk wanna-be. I don't do monk."

"Joe. He sent me orchids today. *Orchids!* With poetry."

To further her fury, he laughed. "All right, all right. You win. You don't know what you're asking."

She knew exactly what she was asking. Hopefully, they could all muddle through this and live happily ever after. Right now she just wanted to focus on one day at a time, and getting Joe in her bed. "It's for a good cause." After all, she didn't want Joe to turn into a grumpy monk.

"Right," he said, sarcasm oozing over the line.

"See you tonight, Joe. I'll bring the movie."

He sighed like he was already missing Monique. "Yeah. See you then."

THAT EVENING, she brought an indie-flick and wore her shortest skirt. If he noticed anything at all, he hid it well. Joe's apartment was exactly as she'd pictured it. There was one overstuffed couch, a leather chair and a coffee table that had never seen a coaster in its carefree existence. No Pottery Barn here. She thought of her own pristine white loft, and sank happily onto the faded cushions. This is what she wanted to understand. How to have a messy life and not feel guilty about it.

"Want something to drink?" He had a beer in one hand, and his shirt hung unbuttoned, as if he had just shrugged into it. She declined the drink and instead handed him the videocassette, secretly studying the chest that he exposed so casually. He was strong, she knew that. He had to be to work on the planes. All muscle, but not bulky. No, long and lean. Bottled energy. When Joe walked, he exuded that energy. She lusted after that energy.

He looked at the tape, a sultry film noir that she thought would be perfect. The sexiest movie she could find that wasn't porn. "You're not going to make celibacy easy, are you?"

She brushed her hair back, and smiled. "Just for a few months. Surely it won't kill you." If she had her way, it'd only be a few weeks. Maybe days. She looked at her watch. Maybe hours.

Joe sank into the big leather chair across from her. Chair and owner immediately became one. She laughed aloud.

He crossed his arms over his chest. "So tell me what you find amusing?"

"I like your furniture."

"Not what you're used to, is it?" There was a defensive note in his voice that she had heard when he was near Avery. He'd never used it around her before now. It hurt her to hear it now, with her.

"Joe, I was being honest. I do like this." She waved her hand around the room. "All of it." A painting hung over the coach and she twisted around for a better look. A naked lady, tastefully done, she'd give him that, but still a nude. She pointed at the pouty raven-haired siren in the picture. "Except for that."

Joe shrugged. "All the blondes hate her. It's art."

"Well, yes, but if you had other pictures..." She stopped and looked around the room. There *were* other pictures. Some landscapes, some portraits and one airplane. "You like art."

"Sue me—" he stopped and held up one hand. "It's only a figure of speech. I never dated a lawyer before. Jeez, I need to watch my mouth."

Still shocked that he liked art, she wasn't even mildly annoyed, only curious. "You don't like lawyers, do you?"

"If I say 'yes,' you'll take it personally, right?"

She nodded.

He thought for a minute, his fingers silently drumming on the chair arm. "Well, you're okay, but you have to admit, most of the personal injury barracudas are annoying as all hell in the commercials."

She agreed with that, but just like everything else, there were good lawyers and there were bad lawyers. She wanted to be one of the good ones. Heck, just two years out of law school and she *was* one of the good ones. "I'm one of the good guys. Truth, justice and corporate responsibility."

"Yeah, but does the job ever get old?"

Sometimes she worried she worked too much. That she was missing something in her life, but her work was important. "Joe, people get hurt every day from things that aren't supposed to hurt them. It's my job to see that not only are people compensated, but more importantly, that corporations change their behavior and that nobody gets hurt anymore."

He smiled. She liked his smile. It was never a grin, but a mere lifting of his lips at the corners. Very Joe. "You're going to be on *60 Minutes* someday, aren't you?"

"I'd like to." She stared at the airplane on the wall. It was an old picture. "It'd be nice to be known for making a mark."

Joe went silent, and too late Amanda realized that she might have said the wrong thing. She changed the subject. "So I'm thinking Avery will show up at nine. What do you think?"

Joe looked silently relieved. "*If* he shows up, it won't be until after *E.R.* It'll take him twenty minutes to get over here, so 11:20."

"Eleven-twenty? Avery's too conscious of appearances to drop in that late, especially unannounced."

His eyes were full of confidence. "Eleven-twenty.

Trust me. You can really set your clock by Avery. I figured that you'd know that by now."

"I've tried to live my life as Avery-free as possible."

"Sorry about that. I've no choice in the matter. But he's okay when you get to know him."

Amanda traced the soft weave of the couch. "It's really not awful. It's not like Avery is a vile parasite. It's just—" she struggled to explain something she didn't understand herself "—I have to be me. Out of everybody, you should understand that best."

He studied her over his bottle. "Who are you?"

Tough question. "I don't know the answer to that yet, but I'm not happy with who I am now."

He took a sip and swallowed. "Thought you'd be over the moon. Making the big bucks, an upstanding young doctor who wants to marry you, you're smart and beautiful. What's not to be happy about?"

"How did you learn to be happy with who you are?"

He did grin this time. "You mean, me, the poor airplane mechanic?"

Oh, right. "You're not poor."

"Maybe not poor, but I don't make half the money you do, honey." He didn't sound like he was joking.

"Really?" She shook her head, not letting him divert her. "You didn't answer my question."

"Why do you think I know the answer?" he shot back.

"Because you do. Aren't you happy with who you are?"

Joe shrugged. "Most of the time."

Most. Surprise number two. She leaned forward, wanting to pry, and he shook his head and picked up the tape. "So, are we really supposed to watch this?"

The easy contentment was back, that quiet peace that made her want to see if his heart was still beating, if his blood could still run so hot. "Unless there's something else you want to do?" She looked at him, trying a sultry, provocative stare, but ended up blushing furiously. Darn. She did not blush well.

Joe watched her for a minute, and tension snapped in the air. Finally he stood and slipped the tape in the VCR. The clock on his VCR was not blinking. She was impressed.

"You sure you don't want something to drink? Water, beer, cola."

Amanda started to refuse, but then changed her mind. "Beer." After all, the purpose of this exercise was to let her hair down a bit. She put a hand to the clip at the back of her head and pulled it free, trying to get eliminate that little bump you get with clip-hair.

Again Joe watched her. Finally he nodded. "I'll get your beer."

While he was gone, she kicked off her sandals, and curled up on the couch. Okay, this was neat. When she was a kid and lived in Queens, she could lie down on the couch. But that all changed after her Dad's big promotion. Her parents now lived in an old renovated farmhouse in Vermont with antiques. No lying down on those things.

A few minutes later he appeared and placed the beer on the coffee table in front of her, and then looked rather determinedly at the television.

"Could you dim the lights a bit?" she asked.

He jerked his head in her direction, and she shrugged apologetically. "You know, in case Avery shows up."

He stood, flipped the light switch, the room turning a deep shade of indigo, the last bit of sun long gone. Joe sat down, looked more determined than ever.

Progress. She crossed her legs at the ankles.

The movie was good. A great mystery, and some very steamy love scenes. She wasn't brave enough to stare meaningfully at Joe during the intimate moments, but she did peek out of the corner of her eye. His jaw looked pretty tight, and there was a bead of sweat on his upper lip.

She shifted a little on the couch, and crossed her legs a little tighter.

When the intercom buzzed, they both jumped. Joe shut off the TV quickly and the room went dark.

Amanda looked at the clock. Eleven-twenty? Already? Gee, time flew when you were watching smut, um, art. "That's Avery, isn't it?"

"Probably," Joe answered.

Avery. Show time. Amanda looked at Joe, shirt untucked, chest untouched, and she glanced down at her own still-ironed look. Even the couch, with all its comfortableness, couldn't lose the starch.

Great. "We don't look like we've been doing anything."

Joe cut his eyes towards her. "Usually women just get this look. Some sort of aura."

She wanted to laugh, but darn it, she needed to think. This was important to get right. "No. Joe, remember this is supposed to be torrid. You need to look like you can't stand one minute without touching me. *Remember*," she stressed the words, "Avery needs to think he doesn't have a chance."

The doorbell rang and Joe lowered his voice to a furious whisper. "This was your idea. What are we supposed to do? Get a little down and dirty on the carpet and just let Avery walk in?"

She looked at the carpet and got a nice visual and decided right then and there that someday indeed she would indeed get down and dirty on the carpet with him.

The doorbell rang, longer this time.

"I'm coming. Just a minute," Joe yelled, still standing several feet away from her, looking completely untorrid.

Amanda took a step toward him. "Look, if this were a real date, what would Avery expect to find?" She wanted to know exactly what was the current fashion for flagrante delicto.

His smile was slow, but smoky. "Babe, if this were real, you'd be lucky to have your socks."

She drowned in the absolute hedonistic waters of his eyes and forgot all about her socks. *Socks*. Heavens. She looked down at her bare feet. She didn't have on socks, did she? She shook her head free of lust. *Not now.* "Okay, here, let me button my shirt up wrong."

She attacked her buttons, Avery now knocking politely but firmly at the door. Well, he could just wait. Very efficiently, she undid the tiny pearl buttons, popping them free. She pulled the stiff cotton material free of her skirt and made the rather huge mistake of looking at Joe.

Her fingers froze. His eyes were leveled on the black satin bra she wore underneath her shirt. Okay, her chest was a little small, but she liked to think of herself as pert.

The way Joe was looking right now, as if she were edible, she was beginning to like pert. Okay, she was beginning to love pert, but she really did need to move her fingers. Unfortunately, every bit of her was paralyzed.

Joe found his tongue, his voice a little hoarse. "You need to button up some of those buttons. I don't think Avery needs to see you looking like that."

She almost reminded him that that was exactly the point, but decided now was not the time to argue. She fumbled for a bit, but the button-loops had mysteriously shrunk two sizes too small, and her hands had grown much more clumsy.

With a muttered curse, he brushed her hands aside and began the task himself.

"Joe, you're buttoning them up right!"

His hands froze. Right on top of her breasts. Oh.

He swore again. One of those fun New Jersey expressions, and then began muttering to himself. "Joe, concentrate. Joe, your brother is at the door." His thumb brushed against her skin.

She jumped. "Joe, you're talking to yourself."

The doorbell rang, longer this time.

Joe looked up, eyes bright with lust. "Don't talk to me right now. I need to just button these damn buttons. What do you have, a million of these tiny things? I told you I don't handle celibacy well."

"How long has it been?" she asked, trying to distract both of them.

"A week."

She groaned.

He gritted his teeth and his finger brushed against her nipple.

She gasped.

Her nipples grew even perkier, clearly visible under the black silk. Joe's breathing turned shallow.

Oh.

Not knowing what else to do, she apologized. "I'm sorry."

He stopped messing with her buttons and focused on her face. A flush ran under his skin, and she no-

ticed where the shadow of whiskers clung to his jaw.
Her fingers lifted, wanting to touch.

"For what?"

She started to explain that she was apologizing for
her nipples and his breathing problem, but realized
this was not what a sultry, provocative seductress
would do. That is, here she stood, her breasts in his
hand, well, almost, and surely she could think of
something.

And so she kissed him.

SHE WAS TRYING to kill him. All that silky white skin.
And her mouth. Now he knew exactly what that
wicked mouth tasted like. Sex. Damn, but if she
didn't kiss better than the best sex he'd ever had. He
pulled her down on the couch and took over, letting
his tongue explore the inside of her mouth. It was
like a drug in his head, and he couldn't breathe. His
hands fumbled with the clasp at the front of her bra
until it broke and feverishly he touched her bare
flesh. He was going to die. He had to—

"Oh, Joe," she sighed in his ear, and he was eter-
nally grateful that at that moment he was named Joe
and not—

The doorbell rang, accompanied by loud knocking. "Amanda! Are you all right?"

Avery.

Joe lifted his head. "Avery, go away!" He stared at
Amanda's face. Fine bones, so delicate. *What was she
doing with him?*

Rational thought returned.

Avery.

He still couldn't look away. She looked almost shocked, her blue eyes still off somewhere about two minutes ago.

He had so needed her to be the sane one. With her body underneath him—how had that happened?—he didn't want to be the sane one. It was physically painful to move off her. "Amanda."

She smiled a little crookedly and sat up. "Joe."

"Amanda, we need to fix your shirt. Avery. I'm sorry."

The fog in her eyes cleared, her focus getting sharper. "Oh." She looked down at the bra now hanging uselessly, then looked up at him and grinned. "Tell you what—" he watched as she pulled the scrap of silk through her sleeves like a magician "—looks better without it anyway. Don't you think?"

Her fingers recovered nicely and she buttoned up a few strategic buttons, but now the bright blue material covered places that he had just seen, conquered.

Unable to do much else, he sat.

Amanda walked to the door, but he ran after he and caught her before she could open it. This was important. There was one question he needed answered.

"Amanda, why did you kiss me?"

"Because..." She hesitated for a long moment and

looked over her fingernails. Finally she looked up at him, eyes big, wide and full of desire. "Because I wanted to."

The doorbell rang and Joe flung it open. Mad at his brother for interrupting, mad at Amanda for starting it and mad at himself for thinking the thoughts that were running in his head. Now he'd really messed up. Now he wanted her.

He look through the open doorway, not really caring about appearances anymore. Avery stood, elegant in a polo shirt and canvas slacks, looking ready for a day on the links. Next to him, in a tight leather miniskirt, scarlet fingernails, stiletto heels and a wisp of a blouse, stood Monique, looking ready to blow.

3

"HELLO AVERY, MONIQUE. I see you two have met." Joe felt like he had an Aerobus engine lodged in his throat.

Avery glowered, a ruddy flush coloring his face. "Joe, I've been waiting *ten minutes*."

"You're lucky it was only ten," Joe replied testily, then shrugged. Now wasn't the time. "Well, come on in."

Monique seemed to be carrying a pot of something that smelled pretty good, and although she tilted her chin in the direction opposite Joe, she followed Avery into the apartment, which seemed to be getting smaller by the minute.

Amanda curled up on the couch again, looking mighty comfortable. Avery sat next to her, and Joe noticed his eyes drifting toward Amanda's cleavage every now and then. If not for Monique, Joe would have kicked him off the couch and told him to get his mind out of the gutter. Unfortunately, Joe had gutter thoughts of his own, and was in no position to throw stones.

He watched as Monique flopped into his favorite

chair. With no other alternative, Joe opted to lean casually against the wall.

There was a long silence, Avery harumphing every now and then, his eyes still darting to Amanda's shirt. Finally, Joe couldn't stand it anymore. "Stop it, Avery."

The remark seemed to work and Avery took out his handkerchief and dabbed at his forehead.

Amanda held out a hand to Monique. "Hi, I'm Amanda." Apparently that was more than Monique could handle.

"Joseph, you told me you were ill. You sounded so sick on the phone, all the coughing and sniffling. I thought I'd find you here, curled at your toilet, miserable, and dying." She held up her pot. "I even brought some of Grandma Steinowitz's chicken soup. It'll have you off your ass in less than twenty-four hours."

"Joe, you cad!" Avery burst out, obviously believing that Monique was not capable of raking Joe over the coals alone.

Joe turned to Amanda and waited. She just sat quietly, holding her tongue. Smart girl. This was her doing. Well, okay, he shouldn't have told Monique he was sick, but how do you call a girl two hours before a date and say, "Um, I've met the woman of my dreams and I won't be seeing you for one hundred and ten days, and about eight hours." Illness seemed so much easier to explain. Of course, he could have told Monique the truth, but what female in their right mind would buy that? Hell, he was a guy, and he wouldn't have believed it.

Joe looked at Monique with a fond sadness. She was nice. He had had high hopes for her, and damn it all, the soup smelled really good. But there was Amanda looking sexy as hell, and a little bit miffed, and he really didn't have a choice. "I'm sorry about this. I should have told you the truth." Joe glared at Amanda at this point. Understanding his message, she slunk a little lower. "To be honest, I just started going out with Amanda and well, it's been something of a shocker." *Especially that kiss.*

Monique sniffed.

Avery was not so shy. "Joe, how could you do such a thing?" He pointed at Amanda. "Are you sure you want to remain in such a shallow relationship? One day, and already he's unfaithful. How could you tolerate such a philanderer?"

Amanda sat up straight, her blouse becoming somewhat less revealing. About time. "Technically, he's not a philanderer."

Monique flipped back a long, brown curl. "Maybe not to you, honey, but you just wait. The girls in Terminal C warned me about this one. Said he was as bad as a pilot working international. And you know how *they* are. He don't have no money, neither. Mechanics never do." She pointed a scarlet-tipped finger at Amanda. "You'll be next, honey. Guys like this—" she clucked her tongue "—worse than rabbits."

Avery patted Monique's hand. "You poor girl. Amanda, if you're ready to leave this little love nest, I'd be more than happy to escort you home." His cool blue gaze cut back to Amanda's cleavage.

Joe allowed himself one proprietary smirk. *Not in your dreams, buddy.*

"I'm not leaving," Amanda stated, in a dreamy voice that reminded Joe that they still needed to lay out a few ground rules before she did really leave. That one kiss might cause him to lose a few nights sleep, but there were some lines he wasn't about to cross. He thought of the kiss again and corrected himself. Okay, he wouldn't cross them more than once.

"Joseph, have you got any brewskis here?" Monique stood up, and pulled at her skirt.

"Amanda, you really should…" Avery began, but then pulled his pager from his pocket. "Blast. I have an emergency at the hospital."

"An emergency?" Amanda asked. "I thought you did mainly cosmetic work?"

Avery puffed up a bit. "Mrs. Corrigan. Dear old lady, but likes to invent a crisis so I can come and chat."

Monique laid a hand on Avery's sleeve. "You're a doctor? So, do you think you could drop me in Astoria on your way? The midnight train is so unpredictable, and those little punkers with the nose rings…" She shuddered.

Joe watched his brother. *Avery in Astoria? Yeah, that'd be the day.*

"Why certainly. You're in such a fragile emotional condition and you don't need to be subjecting yourself to the rigors of public transport."

Well, well. He glanced over at Amanda. Tonight everybody was somebody new.

Monique fluttered a hand over her heart. "It shows? You know, you are *such* a perceptive man. Most of the guys I've dated just miss a woman's little signals. Have you read that Mars Venus book? I just dragged myself out of my well just yesterday." She glanced over at Joe and sighed. "Now, I think me and my well are going to be reacquainted."

Avery took her arm and glared at Joe. "Now look what you've done."

Monique fluttered her lashes at Avery. "Do you drive a Jag?"

"British?" Avery scoffed. "Bavarian Motor Works," he said, opening the door for Monique.

She followed him out, high heels clicking. "What's that?"

"BMW."

Her appreciative "oh" echoed as they walked down the hall. "Like a Bond car."

"One and the same."

"Wow. The girls are never going to believe this...."

Joe heard the tap-tap of Monique's heels as they started down the stairs. One problem solved. Now to tackle the other one. He shut the apartment door and turned to Amanda. "Now, about that kiss..."

Awe-inspiring was the first word that came to Amanda's mind. She already felt like he had ruined her for other men, and she was only thirty. Maybe she'd tire of his kisses in time. She studied his mouth, wondering where he'd learned to kiss like such a professional. "What about it?" she asked, not sure where this conversation was headed.

Joe sat down and rubbed his eyes. For the first time she realized that he looked tired. She resettled herself back on the couch, which was quickly becoming a favorite. Maybe she could give him a massage. Or a hot bath! Amanda loved bubble baths.

"There'll be no more kissing."

That probably meant the bubble bath was out as well, but Amanda wasn't ready to throw in the towel. "You're going to *have* to kiss me. Avery will think something is wrong if you don't even touch me."

"Avery wasn't here," he replied, easily defeating her best argument in defense of kissing.

"Technically, he *was* here."

Joe glared. "In visual range, Amanda."

Amanda adjusted the empty beer bottles on the coffee table. "Semantics, semantics. You will have to kiss me again, or Avery will never be convinced." She narrowed her eyes as another thought struck. "And why did you tell Monique you were sick?

Were you planning on cheating on me?" That thought really hurt. It hurt a lot more than it should. After all, she only wanted an affair.

He leaned forward in the chair. "No, I wasn't planning on..." Then he caught himself. "Damn it, Amanda. This is only pretend." His eyes leveled on her chest. "And button your shirt. Avery's gone. Go home, Amanda. I'll call you a taxi. I need sleep."

Slowly, she buttoned up her shirt, tucking in her shirttail and smoothing out all the wrinkles. Nearly midnight and already her ballgown was transforming back to the norm. She sighed. Well, this was only Day One. And *what* a day it was.

She gathered up her bag and rummaged until she found her keys.

Joe looked in amazement. "You drove?"

Amanda nodded.

"Where'd you park?"

"Down on Riverside."

"Riverside? That's four blocks away. You shouldn't be walking by yourself at night." He stood and stretched, the muscles in his stomach lengthening and flexing. She watched the movement with fevered eyes, wanting to touch. "I'll walk you to your car."

"Thanks."

Neither said much on the walk to the car, and Amanda was happy for the silence. Although his street was anything but—kids were playing basketball, somewhere in the distance a TV was blaring, the sidewalk vibrated from the heavy bass of a nearby low-rider. Two old men were sitting on the stoop, sharing complaints about the neighbors and a bottle in a bag.

The older man was wearing a white undershirt, with tufts of gray chest hair poking out from its edges. His shorts were black polyester, with matching black socks. He took a long swig, and then drew his hand across his mouth. "I was telling the super about that Blazejewski boy just the other day. Remember back—always in trouble that one, I thought he'd never amount to anything. But you know, I saw him yesterday. You'll never believe—he's on the force."

"No! Get outta here," the younger man said. He must have been about seventy and was mostly bald, with a fringe of black circling his head like Friar Tuck.

The old man lifted his right hand. "I swear it's the truth. He had a badge and uniform. Even letting the neighborhood kids fool with the squad car's siren. You should've seen it."

Friar Tuck winked at Amanda. "Good evening, Joseph Barrington. Aren't you going to introduce us to your lady-friend?"

Joe waved them off. "Not tonight, guys."

They joined together in a chorus of catcalls. They looked like such nice men, and Amanda thought it might be rather fun to share a stoop at midnight with Joe.

"Could we sit for awhile?"

Joe's eyes widened. "You want to?"

More than she wanted to go home and be alone. "Sure." She stuck out her hand to older man. "Amanda Sedgewick."

"Vincent D'Antoni," he said, taking her hand and kissing it.

Friar Tuck smiled, exposing sparkling white teeth. How did he manage that? "Bernie Zaluski."

Amanda nodded politely, still wondering about the teeth. Were they dentures? "Very pleased to meet you."

"Charmed, I'm sure." He held out the bag. "Thirsty?"

Amanda glanced over at Joe, who settled himself two steps below the men and shrugged. "Thank you." She sat down next to Joe and took the bag, swallowing one mouthful, and then nearly choked at the chalky liquid. "What is this?"

"Maalox and Schnapps. At my age, you want to save all the time you can." Bernie patted his round stomach.

Joe started to laugh.

"Bernie, mind your manners. A lady is on the stoop tonight." Vincent sighed, wiping his forehead with his handkerchief. "Looks like it's going to be a hot summer."

Bernie handed him the bag. "One of the worst. Remember '83? *Oy*. And the brownouts. I went to bed every night knowing that I'd died and gone to hell."

"If I was married to Edith, I'd think I'd died and gone to hell every night, too." Vincent scratched his chest hair tufts, sighing with satisfaction. "You know, my first child was conceived during those brownouts. God bless her."

"Elizabeth."

Vincent nodded. "The very one." He still had a smile on his face when he turned to Joe. "How's La Guardia Treating you? Where's my Lincoln?"

Joe reached into his wallet and handed over a five-dollar bill. "The actuator. I can't believe you were right. I thought it was the coupler."

"It does my heart good to know an old man can still take advantage of you young whipper-snappers every now and again." Vincent winked at Amanda. "I worked at La Guardia for forty years. Finally retired when Reagan was elected. Joe tell you about his lessons?"

Joe hunched his shoulders over. "Not now, Vincent."

"You haven't told Ms. Sedgewick about your career ambitions?"

Bernie cuffed Vincent on the shoulder. "Vincent. Sshh."

Amanda's ears perked up. "What career aspirations?"

"It's nothing. Vincent," Joe glared meaningfully.

Amanda wasn't going to let Vincent off that easy, though. "Please tell me."

Vincent pursed his lips. "Nope, my loyalty is to Joseph. If he says it's his personal business, who am I to argue?"

Amanda pulled out her wallet. "Vincent, I'd like you to meet Mr. Lincoln." She held out a five.

"Amanda. Put that away." Joe tried to pull her purse away, but she held tight.

Vincent was a tough customer. "Please, miss, listen to him and put that away. I wouldn't rat on our Joseph for anything less than Mr. Jackson."

Everyone laughed.

Amanda looked at Joe for a minute, but he was just watching her. This was a test. She put the money back into her wallet. "Sorry, Vincent."

But then Joe surprised her and told her anyway. "I'm working to get my pilot's license."

She looked at him, amazed. Her hand landed on his knee. "That's great."

"Don't say anything, okay. It's slow going. The hours don't come cheap and it'll be a few years yet before I can fly solo."

He wanted to fly. She shouldn't have been surprised. She had vague memories of Joe as a kid, a toy airplane in his hand.

But he hasn't a kid anymore. Somehow he had grown up and no one had noticed.

Joe stood, tall and capable. Avery had always been the smart Barrington boy, hadn't he? She wasn't so sure now.

Vincent stared up at the looming buildings and incandescent streetlights, looking as if he was contemplating the universe and then he gave a heartfelt sigh. "And what do you do, Amanda?"

"Amanda's a lawyer," Joe answered.

Bernie nudged Vincent. "You don't say? You hear that? She's a lawyer."

Vincent's reply was a noncommittal grunt.

Bernie shook the bag in his hand, pointing it at Amanda. "I've been telling Vincent he should find a good lawyer. Like one of them on TV."

Amanda turned to Vincent, intrigued. "For what?"

"I've been having trouble with my lungs and now nobody's ever said anything, but back when I was on the line, they used this engine cleaner that—well, it was strong stuff, see? They didn't use it very long, but a couple of other guys who did some of the same work at the same time I was there, well, we're all in the same boat."

Bernie sniffed. "They probably knew exactly what they was doing to their employees, but just didn't care. Corporate America. But that's what the legal system is for, to keep them greedy *ganifs* in line."

Vincent looked at Joe. "What do you think?"

Joe shook his head. "You want a lawyer? You're going to need one of the best for a thirty-year-old case."

Amanda opened her mouth, ready to defend her legal skills.

But there was no need. Joe took care of that.

"That's Amanda. Nobody better." His smile was real, but a little sad.

For a moment she just stared. He didn't know what a gift he'd just given her. She should say thank-you, or kiss him, or something, but he had a "hands-off" look. Disappointed, she handed a business card to Vincent. "Call me first thing in the morning. I'll do what I can."

Joe yawned. "Well, I'm sorry to chat and run, but I need to get Amanda back to her car and me to bed."

"Sure, sure," Bernie said as he helped Amanda up from the stoop. "You'd better go. Congressman Lewis is speaking at P.S. 41 tonight on the new park plans and they're still not done debating the location. Four hours! Can you imagine? Plant a tree, four flowers and put a swing set in the middle. It's a park. What? They need a committee to figure this out? When he finally lets them out, traffic's going to be nuts around here."

"Amanda, it was a real pleasure. Good night, Joseph. Come down tomorrow," Vincent said.

"Working midnights tomorrow. Can't do it." Joe stuck his hands in his pockets and turned right at the corner, his stride more a run than a walk.

Amanda waved to the old men and then hustled to keep up. "Joe, wait. Why didn't you tell me about the flying lessons? That's so great."

He stopped, his eyes hard. "Look. Nobody knows. Okay. I don't know if I'll be able to finish or not. I don't know if I *want* to finish. It's a lot more than I can handle." He pointed to the row of cars parked on the street. "Which one is yours?"

She almost didn't tell him. "The Mercedes."

He just shook his head and laughed. "Yeah, why didn't I guess?" She unlocked it with her remote, and he opened the door for her.

"See you around, Amanda." He started to turn away.

"Wait." She leaned against the cool steel door, shutting it. "What do we do now?"

"We've already done too much."

In Amanda's mind, they hadn't done nearly enough, but she kept her mouth shut. "I'm talking about Avery."

"Why don't you marry him, Amanda? I've never seen two people more perfect for each other. My parents would be thrilled." He actually sounded serious.

Why couldn't anyone understand? "My plan is working. Avery really believes we're having an affair. Just a little while, Joe. Give it a chance. I need your help."

"Amanda, you don't need anyone's help. Least of all, mine. You could do anything you set your mind to."

She didn't want to see him go. Not yet. "Please? I know this will work."

Joe looked up at the streetlights and closed his eyes. "Why would Avery ever believe this?"

It was the sarcastic tone that made her angry. "Look at me. I have put up with Avery Barrington for twenty-one years! That's longer than most marriages. For the first time, Avery is actually entertaining thoughts of other women. Did you see him with Monique? That is what I was trying to tell you. This is going to work. It's got to work. I don't know what else to do." To her chagrin, she felt tears pricking at the corner of her eye and she dashed them away with the back of her hand.

Joe swore, lifted a hand to touch her, and then stopped. "Don't start crying. Look, if you want me to help, I'll help." He pushed at his dark hair with an unsteady hand. "But nothing else, Amanda. I don't know exactly what you're thinking here, but he's my brother. Nothing is going to happen between us." He shoved his hands in his pockets and took a step back. "Nothing."

Amanda knew when it was time to pull back. She opened the car door, and settled in the plush, leather interior. Why couldn't she drive a Volkswagen? He shut her door and saluted. Completely unaffected by what she considered was certainly a defeatist attitude, Amanda rolled down the window and waved. "You work on Sunday? We can go dancing."

Joe put a protesting hand on the car door. "What if Avery won't show?"

That she ignored, pulling away from the curb, honking her horn. Just to make sure he understood, she stuck her head out the window. "I'll be by your place at eight o'clock to pick you up. Don't be late."

She glanced in her rearview mirror and watched

Joe get smaller and smaller as she drove away. Well, their first date had gone surprisingly well, considering it was a disaster.

Sunday would be their Day Two. She touched her lips, remembering his kiss...touched her breast, remembering his touch, and then smiled to herself. He inspired such passion in her. Passion she'd never felt before. And who would have thought that Amanda Sedgewick would be out at midnight, sitting on a stoop in the heart of the city? It felt good.

An affair with Joe would be all that she imagined. *And more.*

4

AT JOE'S INSISTENCE, they took a cab. Some termed a New York cab living dangerously, however Amanda had always secretly loved it. Their cab driver was Armando Cruz, licensed since August 31, 2001. His Yankee's cap was turned backward in what Amanda termed the doofus look.

"Where to, man?"

"137 Eighth Avenue. Brooklyn."

Armando looked at Joe in the rearview mirror. "You're sure about that?"

Joe nodded.

The cab lurched forward, pealing away from the curb. "Brooklyn it is."

Amanda found herself flat against the seat and laughed in delight. "Step on it, Armando."

Joe's blue gaze flickered over in her direction, and she felt a fresh burst of heat wash over her skin.

He liked her dress.

Oh, he hadn't said a word, but the banked appreciation in his eyes spoke volumes. Every now and then, they would drift in her direction, as intimate as a touch.

She shivered.

"Cold?" he asked, glancing at her chest.

She fought the urge to cross her arms over her breasts, and instead smoothed the red silk material lovingly over her thighs. She watched with smug confidence as he turned a little paler. "No, thank you for asking."

The cab lurched left again, spoiling her moment.

The deserted midtown streets slid by, although every now and then an evening jogger or dog-walker would appear. Amanda checked her watch. Eight-thirty. If she was back by one, she could finish going through the articles she'd found on industrial cleaning solvents and their side effects. She'd agreed to take Vincent's case almost immediately after they talked on Friday, and after two solid days of research she knew she was on to something.

And Joe didn't miss a thing. "Got someplace else you want to be?"

She smiled and shook her head. He was exactly what she needed. Dressed in slacks and a plain cotton shirt, his hair slightly mussed, and a wicked gleam in his eye, he looked—perfect. "No. Tonight I'm going out on the town. It's playtime."

His eyes locked with hers for a moment, and then he turned away, looking out the window instead.

Chicken.

As they drove through Little Italy, there were pasta shops everywhere. She could imagine the smell of freshly baked bread and sauce simmering in garlic. Under the shimmering glow of the streetlights, two young lovers walked hand in hand. Amanda sighed, the long-forgotten echoes of Frank Sinatra playing in her head.

The cab screeched around a corner and Amanda slid into Joe. Mysteriously, her hand found its way to his thigh. Not so mysteriously, her hand worked its way up his thigh.

Joe didn't blink. "You don't want to be doing that."

"Oh, yes I do." He sat straight, taut, very unlike the easygoing man she thought she knew. Amanda plunged forward. "You're attracted to me."

He shrugged. "You're a female. You're alive. I'm easy."

A headache throbbed right between her eyes. She had known he was stubborn. Had always thought his "stick-to-his-guns" trait was appealing, attractive even. She was an idiot. She rubbed the bridge of her nose. "We don't have to pretend, Joe."

"Yes. We do."

She flashed him a gentle, comforting smile. "No. We don't."

"Yes. We do."

Amanda moved in closer. "We could do torrid, you know."

"No."

"Hot." She licked her lips, getting into this femme fatale persona. The courtroom had never been this exciting.

"No." The denial sounded a little strained.

"I could make you forget your name."

"You're Avery's girl. That's all I need to remember."

The mood shattered. "I'm Amanda Jocelyn Sedgewick. Daughter of Richard and Leona Sedgewick. Graduate, magna cum laude, of Columbia University, and Cornell University law. I'm my own person. Not Avery's girl."

They drove over the Brooklyn Bridge, and Joe looked away staring at the dark waters of the East River. The full moon cast a silver glow over the bridge's spider-webbed cabling. "He's in love with you."

"Fixated. Avery's love affair with himself is bigger than me, bigger than both of us."

He turned back towards her and smiled. "Yeah."

"You're stubborn."

His smile turned cocky and sure. "Just like my big bro."

Her leg began to shake. She'd never quite been able to conquer the spasm of agitation, but she could hide it. She leaned back against the seat, tucking one ankle behind the other. Her voice was not all fun and games. "Why did I ever have to meet the Barringtons?"

"You're cursed," he replied, looking completely serious.

"You think Avery will be there tonight?"

"Yeah, I told him we were going dancing. He knows where I go."

The driver turned his head and winked at Amanda. "137 Eighth Avenue. Twelve dollars and seventy-five cents."

Joe fished in his wallet and paid the driver, and then held the door open for Amanda.

But Armando wasn't done. "Hey if my girl looked like she does, and if my girl wanted to dance with me like that, I wouldn't be in no cab. I'd be giving her the Armando Mambo. You're a loser, *man.*" He pointed a finger at Joe to emphasize the words.

Amanda winked at the cabbie. "He's not really a loser, just a little hesitant."

"Lady, you need a real man? You come to Armando. I'll treat you good."

"Get out of the car, Amanda."

She emerged from the cab, haughty and professional. "You are no gentleman, Joe."

"Nag, nag, nag." He slammed the door behind her.

Her heels sounded as she made her way down the street. "But I'm still gonna make you forget your name."

THIS CLUB has always been Joe's favorite place. Unassuming and out of the way, no one ever made judgments. The music was dark and sexy, just like the air. Blue Velvet was a throwback to days gone by, and for Joe, it was the best place to meet women.

But tonight, he was playing white knight for Amanda. And he wasn't a loser. That one remark from Armando had hurt more than all the digs against his testosterone levels. He had spent his life not measuring up to Avery, and eventually he stopped trying. But with Amanda? Damn. For her, he wanted to try again. Those thoughts of material success were weaving a spell in his head.

Joe leaned back against the stuffed cushions of his seat. He sipped his beer and let the music wash over him. He'd already played that game once. Not again.

Not even for Amanda.

He watched as she moved on the dance floor. The red dress billowed out and then flowed back as she swayed to the sultry sounds of Nina Simone.

What was she doing with him? Why this sudden desire to walk on the wild side? Amanda was a high-society type. About as stuffy as Avery and just as polished and refined. That's what prep school did to people. Probably was a good thing Joe didn't go. He didn't want to be polished, didn't want to be refined.

His eyes narrowed, watching her move. Maybe not so stuffy after all.

He should be dancing with her. Instead, like a big jerk-off, he'd said no. And now, she was swirling on the dance floor with four guys flocked around her like an entourage in a music video.

Way to go, Joe.

He looked at his watch. Ten-thirty. Avery would be here soon. Joe would have to hold Amanda close, kiss that mouth again, kiss all that white silky skin.

Why did he ever agree to this?

Because you wanted to, sap, a voice whispered in his head.

One of the big bruisers pulled Amanda closer and Joe put down his beer. He stalked out on the dance floor, grabbed Amanda, and spoke very clearly to all the hulking members of her entourage.

"She's mine."

Amanda's body locked up against his and he sucked in every molecule of oxygen, causing his head to spin.

She looked up at him, lashes fluttering, red silk barely covering the shadowy cleavage he still remembered touching. Her eyes were dancing with misguided hero-worship. He definitely wasn't a loser. Not tonight.

"Is Avery here?"

"No." Joe moved his feet, found the slow, throbbing beat, and maneuvered her around the floor.

She perked up. "You did that on your own? Because you wanted to?" Her hands curled into his hair. "Maybe you should kiss me, too."

He wanted to do a lot more than kiss her. He wanted to take her home, peel the red silk from her skin, bury himself inside her for days. He looked up at the door, saw the full frontal protrusion of Avery's jaw, and smiled tightly. "Maybe I should."

He stopped moving, and met her waiting lips. He had hoped, he had prayed that his memories were faulty, that he'd built her up to be some sort of fantasy, but when he felt her lips melt under his tongue, he realized the reality was even sweeter. She tasted so good, so exotic, so ripe. Her tongue mingled with his, moving back and forth in his mouth, making love to him with her mouth, all in time to the music. He drew her closer, until their bodies merged together. For a moment, he let himself forget, but only for a moment. He drew back, stared into her eyes, wanting to understand her.

"Why are you doing this to me?"

"Because I like you," her lips nuzzled his jaw, "you're sexy as hell," her hands skimmed his back, "and I desperately want your brother to leave me alone."

He took her hands in his, needing to have her stop touching him. He couldn't think. "It doesn't have to be real."

That sultry smile could have overheated any engine. He didn't *even* want to think about what it was doing to his own less-stablized anatomy. "I want it to be real."

He locked his hands behind his back. Much safer. "Why?"

"I want to feel. I want passion. I want...more than what I have now. You could teach me."

Fantasies popped into his head. Vivid portrayals of naked flesh, long blond hair and her mouth. On him. Oh, God. Could he teach her? He coughed, his desire to breathe momentarily forgotten. He had to get control of the situation. He was losing it. "There's at least four other guys, five if you count Armando, who would be more than happy to teach you how to have passion in your life."

Her gaze was only for him. "And what about *you?*"

"I can't argue with any lawyer." He stepped back away from her, before he touched her again. Before he forgot all about why they were doing this. Before he forgot all about Avery.

Those eyes that had flashed hero-worship before now flashed with anger and she grabbed his arm. "Now's not the time, Joe. There's Avery." She tilted her head toward the door. "At least pretend."

Pretend. He could do that. He watched as his brother found a table and ordered a vodka martini—shaken, not stirred. Joe knew the drill. Joe pulled Amanda close, smelled her perfume—what was she wearing?—and saw his brother's eyes narrow.

What was he doing?

Amanda pulled away and danced a tight circle around him, teasing, taunting, pursing her wicked mouth, sending him imaginary kisses. His body was not happy with imaginary; it wanted the real deal. He looked at Avery, who had now looked away.

Damn.

Amanda was just Amanda. This wasn't supposed to hurt Avery. Hell, nothing hurt Avery. At least not anymore. Avery had done all he set out to do, except for one thing. Marrying Amanda—the most amazing woman that Joe had ever met.

Her hair swirled around her, brushing his arm, his face.

Suddenly Joe didn't want to do this. He just wasn't that low.

"I can't."

Her smile turned slow and confident. A seductress. She took his hand and pulled them off the dance floor. They walked a few steps to the narrow hallway where autographed pictures of old musicians hung in tribute.

In the dim light, her smile lost a little wattage, became a little less sure. "Joe, you're the only one who can fix this."

"Find some other way. Did you see the way's he's looking at you? I'm not like you. I can't ignore that. Talk to him. Dump him yourself."

"I've tried."

"Try harder."

They could have heard her snarl in Jersey. "If I talked to him, and he still believes I'm his soul mate, *then* will you agree?"

"How will I know you're really trying? I don't trust you, Amanda."

She threw up her hands and he caught a glimpse of a white breast, the shadow of her nipple. God, how he wanted he wanted to touch her.

"Listen. Decide for yourself. I'll invite Avery over for drinks after work on Monday, and you can hear the whole thing."

"Eavesdrop?" He frowned.

"You said you didn't trust me."

"I don't."

"Do you see another way?"

Joe wished for a flash of inspiration, but in the back of his mind he wanted nothing more than to see her tomorrow. "No."

"Fine. Show up tomorrow at seven. My place."

"Better make it eight. Avery likes *Dateline*."

She closed her eyes, the picture of a sexy woman, desperately needing a white knight. "Fine," she said, sounding so tired.

His heart twisted.

He headed out of the bar and he barely gave a nod to his brother on the way out, his stomach cramping like he'd had too much to drink. He didn't trust himself with alcohol around Amanda. It wouldn't take much to send him over the edge, and he suspected she knew it.

Amanda meant trouble. Somewhere about the time that Joe got his mechanics license, he discovered that he was content with his life. He liked his neighborhood and he had his friends. At last he'd found where he belonged. But every time he looked at Amanda, every time she watched him with that cool, appraising gaze, he felt anything but content.

He wanted to leap over tall buildings in a single bound or astound her with his captivating wit. Neither of which was very likely. There was only one superhero in the Barrington family. Avery.

He saw her to her building—some high-rise in a part of town that he had long forgotten. Time to go home, time to get drunk, time to wish he was somebody else besides Avery Barrington's brother.

5

BRIGHT AND EARLY Monday morning, Grace knocked discreetly and then entered Amanda's office sporting her latest eyewear—red plastic frames trimmed with U.S. flags at the sides. On anyone else, it might have been silly, but the office temp wore Old Glory quite well.

"Hey boss. Barrington's on line three."

Amanda's fingers froze over her keyboard. "Joe?" she asked, trying to hide her eagerness.

"Nah. It's the doctor." Grace sat on the edge of Amanda's desk; her assignment was only three weeks ago and already she was at home. "You know, boss, I can't see why you're so taken with this Joe person. Now, this doctor, he's the one. He sent you orchids again, by the way. They're in the lobby. Want me to get them?"

Amanda pulled off the glasses she used for her reading. "Don't you have anything better to do?" Amanda handed her the trashcan filled with two pieces of paper. "Here, shred this."

"Boss, boss, boss." The young girl clicked her tongue, her dark curls flying as she shook her head. "You know, we females are just so blind when love is involved. There's nothing to be ashamed of. Take a look at the facts. Your doctor calls at least twice a week—" she lowered her voice "—and I don't think Joe has called once since I've been working the phones."

The truth really hurt. In Joe's eyes, she was off-limits, and she might as well have been stamped with a big, red X.

Why did she want an affair with him so badly? Was it the challenge? The need to succeed at every-thing she did? She touched her spotless desk with the two pens poised carefully in their proper places, and longed for disorder.

"The Doc?" Grace pointed a finger at the blinking light on the phone.

Amanda shook off her own version of personality trait hell and shot her temp a "get lost" glance. Which did absolutely no good. What did it matter anyway?

She picked up the phone. "Avery?"

"Amanda. Just wanted to make sure you received a delivery. Besides, the dulcet tones of your voice just brighten my day so."

Amanda sighed. "Avery, I was going to call you so I'll get right to the point."

"Of course, with time as valuable as yours, chit-chat should be kept to a minimum."

"Avery, could you come over this evening?"

"But of course! Is something wrong? Did Joe do something to hurt you? I knew that nothing good could come of this—"

"No, Avery. I just think we need to talk. Maybe seven?"

"Could we make it eight?"

"Dateline?"

"You watch it as well? They're doing a piece next week on Johns Hopkins. I've always wanted to lecture there."

Amanda smiled. Avery wanted to save the world, Joe wanted to fly around it and neither one of them was close. What a pair. "See you tonight, Avery."

"I'll bring a bottle of wine. Rothschild perhaps. Must go. The hospital's paging me. See you tonight then."

Grace looked at Amanda, a broad grin splitting her face. She held up one hand, a waiting high-five gesture. Trying to get in the spirit, Amanda responded, albeit a little half-heartedly.

Grace didn't notice and jumped right in. "The rose silk."

Amanda had no idea what that meant. "Pardon?"

"You need to wear the rose silk you wore last week for the staff meeting. It's so classy, but kinda sexy, too. You know?" The girl's leg idly bumped against in the desk with an annoying thump-thump sound.

"I'll take it under advisement." Amanda slid her glasses back on her nose. "Why don't you hand me the D'Antoni file and then get out of here? I have a lot of calls to make."

"Sure thing, boss." Grace delivered the case file then left, sighing heavily.

Finally.

Amanda lifted her receiver once more. This time to call Joe. She stared at the two pens, standing upright in their holder, a perfect ninety degrees. With quiet determination, she took one and laid it flat on the middle of her desk.

"There."

Joe came on the line, the usual noises rang in the background.

"Barrington."

Amanda twisted the pen, spinning it on her desk. "It's Amanda. Avery will be at my place at eight. You'll be there?"

"I'll be over at five til."

He couldn't stand to be around her just one extra moment. Grace was right, she was a fool. "I'll see you then. Bye, Joe."

But he had already hung up.

After staring at the pen for a good three minutes, she blew out a breath and then put it back in its holder, propping it upright until it was perfectly aligned with the other.

Last night, as they had danced so slowly, Joe had given her a long, wet kiss as if she were the only woman alive. As if he needed her more than air. Amanda's life was planned and premeditated. She didn't understand need like that, but it drew her to him. She hadn't known it until now, but it was everything she always wanted.

"EXCUSE ME, MARGE. I've been on hold for some time now. I really don't want to hold anymore." Amanda looked at the notepad full of drawings and sighed. She'd spent the last ten minutes on hold drawing pictures of ballpoint pens. She really needed to get out more.

"I work very hard, Ms..... What did you say your name was, Ms.?"

"Sedgewick. Amanda Sedgewick. Look, I know you work very hard and all, but I need to know who was Mr. Lowenthal's secretary in 1971." She put the pen back in the holder. No more doodling.

"Clean-All has lots of records, Ms. Sedgewick. You'd have to submit a written request—"

"Yes, of course I know you have a lot of records, but I'm sure that somewhere, somehow, someone can find this out for me. Perhaps if I came to your office and waited."

"That information is at the warehouse. And then there was the merger in '83, and I think those personnel records might have been lost."

Amanda removed the newspaper article from the folder and scanned the text quickly. Lowenthal was mentioned, along with Boswick. "How about Mr. Boswick? Is he still working there?"

"Oh, no. He got laid off in, um, let me see, must have been about 1994, maybe '95."

"Do you know how I can find him?"

"Boswick? Last I heard he was heading up the Operations Division for Atlantic Industries."

Amanda's ears perked up. "Atlantic?" She'd met with them just last year over a workers comp case.

She riffled through her Rolodex. *A*. Atlantic Industries.

"Yes indeed. Got a sweet deal when he left, too."

"Thanks Marge. If you ever need a lawyer, you let me know."

Amanda hung up the phone and leaned back in her chair. D'Antoni case. Day Four. Progress.

Now she just needed to track down Boswick at Atlantic Industries. She took one last look at the old newspaper headline—Airline Lawsuit Settled—before folding it and putting it in her briefcase. The sun was starting to lower in the office window and she realized it must be later than she thought. She checked her watch—five-thirty. Darn. She could at least call Boswick and see if he left the office for the day. And she needed to spruce up the apartment before Avery came over. And Joe. Before Joe came over.

That brought a smile to her face. She had big plans for Joe Barrington this evening.

She straightened up her desk and put D'Antoni's file in her briefcase. She'd take that home with her. She could call Boswick from her cell phone on the way home.

FOR SOME unexplained reason, Joe found himself at her door at seven-fifteen. He rang the bell, refusing to analyze his motive for showing up early, refusing to admit that maybe he did want to see her before Avery got there.

She opened the door, her hair wrapped in a white

towel, her body wrapped in a long, white satin robe. Her smile alone made the visit worth it. "Come on in. Sorry. I'm running a little late. Work. It never stops."

He followed, watching her satin-covered butt, wondering what she was wearing underneath it. No panty-lines whatsoever. His heart skipped a beat, the rest of him cheered as well.

She didn't say anything about him being early, thank God, because he didn't have any answers.

"I'm just getting dressed. You want something to drink?"

He shook his head.

"I was thinking you could wait in the bedroom while Avery's here. If I leave the door open, you can hear everything that's being said."

Joe's thoughts slammed back to the present, unpleasant situation. He wasn't CIA or FBI. "Look, Amanda, I shouldn't be here. This is just silly."

She put her hands on her hips. "This is what you wanted."

Point for the lawyer. "Well, yeah, but I was...you know, not right." Her head tilted, the towel balancing nicely. How did women do that?

"Wrong? Is that what you're trying to say? Wrong about what, Joe?"

Admitting being wrong did not come easy to Joe, and he thought, preparing a response, wanting to help her, wanting to look intelligent, but not ready to commit himself too far. It was a guy thing. "Tonight. You don't have to do this. I was pissed and I should have just shut up. You don't have to prove anything to me." He stayed silent for a minute. Finally, he said that words that he'd come to say. "I trust you."

That brought a smile to her face. He really liked it when she smiled. *Really* liked it when he made her smile.

"Why the change of heart?" she asked quietly.

"Avery called. He wanted to know what I'd done to you."

Amanda muttered something Joe couldn't hear, but he didn't think Avery would be flattered. "I told him you hadn't done anything."

Joe brushed it off with laughter. "It's all right. He's used to thinking the worst." *Usually Avery was right.* "He's just concerned. He doesn't want me to hurt you."

Amanda sat down on her couch, crossed her legs. "This is between me and you, not Avery."

Joe eyed her bare thigh peeking out from under her robe and imagined how it would feel wrapped around him. "Amanda," he said, in what was supposed to be a warning. Instead it sounded like a plea.

"Yes?" She looked up at him, all innocence. Like she didn't know exactly what was going on in his head.

Somehow he needed to get back to the subject at hand. "Look, Amanda. Talk to Avery. I'll stay out of sight. If he doesn't see sense, after he leaves, we'll get that robe off—"

Joe bit his tongue. Hard.

Amanda stood up and walked toward him, her hands at the tie on her waist. "If you want—"

"Gee, look at the time! You better get dressed." He pulled her into her bedroom. "Unless you want Avery seeing you...seeing you..." *looking like every guy's favorite fantasy.* He waved his hand. "Like that."

Amanda smiled again, this one a little more confident than the last. Just what he needed. "You're right." She smiled. "Anything you want to watch while I'm getting dressed?"

His gaze flew up to meet her eyes before he realized she was talking about the TV that sat on her dresser. *Pervert.* "I'll be fine."

Without a word, she handed him the remote and departed to the confines of her closet, which appeared to be as big as his whole apartment.

He glanced around the room. Bed, dresser, big mirror over dresser.

She emerged three minutes later with a dress hooked over her arm. Lace scraps dangled from her hand and he swallowed. He really did *not* need to see her underthings. She headed for the bathroom behind him, and called over her shoulder, "I'll only be a minute. Make yourself comfortable."

Comfortable? She was just in the other room—naked, al fresco, bare, nude—he was in her bedroom, alone with her bed—he glanced at the Big Beast and laughed.

He should have known. It was a full-size bed with

at two pillows that looked as if they'd been pressed and plumped.

Her comforter was a soft white thing and he was able to handle everything until he noticed the sheets peeking out from the corner.

Satin. White.

Geez. A part of him wanted to run screaming from the room. He'd never slept in satin sheets before, but suddenly his mouth was watering at the thought of doing just that. He collapsed on the bed and fingered the silky material.

Amanda slept here. Probably in some slinky lace teddy thing that cost more than one of his paychecks.

That was the way Amanda would make love. Silk, satin, candlelight and flowers. That's the woman she was.

He stared at his reflection in the mirror, sitting on her bed like he belonged there. When they made love, every movement, every image would be vibrantly available right in front of his eyes.

God, he was getting hard. It was so easy to imagine.

She seemed so vivid, so real. All that white satin flesh reflected in front of him. A heart-shaped butt that was perfectly symmetrical. His hands clenched. She brushed out her hair, her arms raised, her breasts firm and uplifted. She looked more like one of those great Italian sculptures—Bernini's Daphne—than a living, breathing woman.

Somewhere in the distance he heard a whimper.

Yup, that was him all right. Weak, Barrington, very weak.

He rubbed his eyes, willing the fantasy away. But when he opened them again, she was still there, and that's when it clicked. This was no fantasy. She *was* real, and he was sitting here, watching her reflection in the mirror.

Some bit of suspicion popped into his head. Was this on purpose? Another trick to get him into her bed? He looked down, noticed the way his jeans were suddenly four sizes too tight and admitted her trick was working.

Nah. He'd been watching too many conspiracy movies. Instead of playing the voyeur-extraordinaire, he should be watching TV. He leaned back against the pillows, pressed the On button and tried to concentrate on the images. It was a wasted effort.

TV was boring. Amanda getting dressed was not. And what would it really hurt? Hell, she *had* probably planned the whole thing.

His eyes, happy to be relieved of any guilt, cut back to the pure perfection of Amanda Sedgewick's body. Her skin was so fair it was almost silver. She started to apply lotion to her body, her hands smoothing, touching, and in his mind he started to mimic her movements, as if he were rubbing her down.

She turned sideways, and sucked in her breath, patting her stomach, and Joe smothered his laughter. No, she didn't know she was being watched.

At that exact moment, she lifted her head, and got

a good long look at Joe Barrington in her mirror, eyes hot, jaw tense and mouth slightly open.

Busted.

He couldn't look away and she didn't even try. Her head tilted, a question in her eyes. Her fingers splayed on her stomach and then they moved. First up, to cover her breasts, almost in modesty, but mostly in seduction. Her fingertips trailed over her nipples, and he groaned.

She smiled, slow and aware, and her hands moved down, lower, lower. He rose, not thinking about any of the reasons he shouldn't be doing this, and started toward her. All he wanted to do was to taste her skin, kiss that sinful mouth and tease the places that would make her scream.

He was halfway across the room and the intercom buzzer blasted above the sound of his own tortured breathing.

Avery.

Joe closed his eyes and found a chair in a far corner of the room. Far away from temptation, far away bedroom tricks with mirrors. A few seconds later, Amanda walked out of the bathroom, safely dressed in peach silk, her hair pulled back away from her face and twisted up on her head. She looked elegant, untouchable, and completely forbidden.

"Joe?"

"Go buzz him up." His voice was hoarse and he had trouble forming words.

She didn't respond, just stared for a minute. After

three heartbeats, she turned away and walked out the room.

AMANDA'S LEGS were unsteady, but they carried her to the front door. She pressed the button to let Avery in and then rested her head against the door. She was turning into an exhibitionist and my, it was quite... stimulating.

If not for Avery's untimely arrival, she knew exactly what would have happened.

It thrilled her to realize how close they had come and a part of her body was still humming, waiting for a release. Maybe he would stay after Avery left; maybe he would see how futile it would be to keep fighting the sparks between them. Maybe he would now understand that Amanda Sedgewick could tease and tempt just as well as any female that he might have favored in the past.

Maybe he could like her.

Avery knocked at the door, eliminating any more thoughts of a late-night seduction. First things first.

Dealing with Avery.

6

AVERY ALWAYS LOOKED so well-pressed. Amanda stared down at her own wrinkle-free silk, and grimaced. "Please, come in."

He bowed low from the waist and brought forth a bottle from behind his back. "A rare vintage for the rarer flower."

From her bedroom, she heard a muffled cough and she was glad she'd left the TV on.

"Avery, sit down."

Obediently, he sat and then pulled a bottle opener from his jacket and proceeded to start uncorking the wine. "I brought everything but the goblets."

She nearly ran to the kitchen, finding two crystal glasses. When she entered the living room once more, he was sniffing the cork appreciatively. With a loud clank, she placed them on her Danish modern coffee table, then seated herself on a chair that was a safe distance away. Not rude, but not encouraging, either.

He poured her a bit, then poured some in his own glass. "A toast."

She didn't lift her glass, but did place a wooden

coaster underneath it. Just in case. "Avery, wait. You may not want to toast after what I've got to say."

He cocked his head, his eyes curious and empathetic. The perfect doctor. "Yes? Please, say what's on your mind."

She folded her hands in her lap, the single frayed fingernail carefully hidden away. "Avery, I know you think you care for me, but I don't think you really do...."

"Is this why you're taking up with Joe, to make me jealous?"

"No, Avery. That's not why."

"Amanda, you've always been there on the fringes of my life. Ready to defend me when others wouldn't dare. I've always believed you cared for me."

"And I do. But as a friend. Is that what you want? You deserve much more."

He took her hand, the one with the bad fingernail. "Having you, even just in friendship, makes me happier than being with any other woman who sees me as nothing more than a bank account."

She stared into his warm blue eyes and wished she were the woman for him. He deserved someone good, nice, the perfect wife. Someone who could love him for every pompous, stuffy inch of him. "I wouldn't be happy with friendship and you know, deep down, you wouldn't either."

"I don't know, Amanda. You're a wonderful woman, I think we're well-suited."

"You think you know who I am, but you would be miserable with me."

"Why do you say that?"

She removed her hand. Took a much needed sip of wine. "I'm cold and heartless. I'm not pleasant when I don't get my way."

"Well, all women have their days."

Her hand tightened around the stem of the glass. His lady-killer skills were lacking. Sadly lacking. "That's a very sexist remark."

"My apologies, of course."

"Avery, we're not meant for each other. I want to feel alive, I want to make a difference. I don't feel that way when I'm with you."

"And you do with Joe?"

She nodded. It was the truth.

"Why?" he asked.

More doctor questions. *Good grief.* "You're not making this easy."

"To put it quite succinctly, I think you're trying to dump me, so I don't have an obligation to make things *easy.*"

"I'm not trying to dump you. That would imply that something existed between us that never actually did. And never will. You're a dear, dear, man—"

Avery cut her off at the pass. "You take your time, Amanda. We're alike, you and me. Certainly more than you and Joe. You're sophisticated, intelligent, ambitious."

Amanda removed her hand. "And you don't think Joe is?"

"My brother always did things his own way. He's certainly not sophisticated, his intelligence, or lack of it, is the reason he didn't go to school with you and me, and ambitious? What do you think, Amanda?"

"I don't understand how you two can be brothers and be so completely opposite. You lack some of Joe's better qualities, Avery."

Avery shrugged, just like Joe. "All these years, Amanda, why did you stay my friend? I'd always assumed you had feelings for me. Were those feelings of sympathy?"

He looked at her, completely clueless. That was Avery. "No. I just saw things inside you that the other kids didn't. I saw your potential."

"Potential?" His laugh wasn't pretty. "I was a project to you then? Science fair? Make the mouse into a man? You want to change the whole world, don't you? Is Joe next on your list?"

That brought her to her feet. "You will not twist this around to suit you. Avery, what is between us is friendship, nothing more. It never will be."

Silence overwhelmed the room, and for the first time, Avery Barrington, III looked beaten. "And that's it, isn't it?"

She cleared her throat. "Let me find someone for you, Avery. I have some friends who would love to meet you."

His mouth twitched with amusement. "A date? You want to play matchmaker?"

"Yes. A novel concept. Fairly underutilized by the male sex, but quite effective. Would you let me?"

He struggled for words for a moment, adjusting his tie, taking a sip of wine. "What sort of woman do you envision for me?"

"Someone who would set the perfect table, have her hair perfectly coiffed, would have a warm cup of tea waiting for you when you get home."

His smile seemed quite genuine. "It does sound quite appealing." But then he frowned. "You would go with us, though?"

One step at a time, Amanda. One small step at a time. "With Joe, of course." Again, the muffled cough from the bedroom.

Avery turned his head. "What *is* that noise?"

"The television."

"Amanda, Amanda, Amanda..." Avery heaved an elaborate sigh. "He's here, isn't he? My rival, my blood, my brother." Avery stood up. "Joe! You letch, show yourself!"

Joe appeared in the doorway to the bedroom, looking quite at home. Amanda was pleased. "Does anybody say 'letch' besides you?"

"There's other terms, but I'm in the presence of a lady."

Joe heaved an elaborate sigh, sounding just like his brother. Amanda studied him carefully, trying to decide if he was mocking Avery. But no, he didn't even seem to know he did it.

She watched the undercurrents between the two men, not sure what to do. "Joe, would you like some wine?"

He smiled at her. A nice smile. A supportive smile. She really liked that smile. "Nah. I'll just get a beer." He strolled into the kitchen, again looking quite at home. Avery frowned.

Did she have beer in the refrigerator? Amanda thought for a moment, not sure that she did. But then Joe came from the kitchen, with a beer bottle in his hand. Well, she must have bought some. Joe sat down on the arm of her chair. Casual, possessive, and enough to cause a hot shiver to run down Amanda's back. Was he changing towards her?

Joe tilted his bottle at his brother. "Avery, back off."

Well, she certainly hadn't expected that, but his defense was nice. Avery's well-sculpted eyebrows rose a fraction of an inch. "Are you threatening me?"

Joe spoke with the lifelong weariness of a younger brother. "No, I'm not threatening you. I'm trying to help you."

"What can you do to help me?" Avery asked with all the superiority of an older brother.

Amanda leapt to Joe's defense. "Avery, be nice."

Joe gave her a nice little hug for her effort. "You need to meet other women, Avery. Get out, do things. Live a little."

"Like you do, you mean."

"Exactly."

Avery huffed. "I would never—"

"Joe's right," Amanda interrupted.

Avery looked at her as if she had suddenly turned into an Unidentified Female Object. "Do you really think so?"

Avery looked so earnest that Amanda felt a pang of sympathy. "That's what I've been trying to tell you."

Joe leaned forward, putting the cool bottle against Amanda's neck, a gesture that his brother noticed. She felt the cold sweat trickle down her neck and she crossed her legs tighter, squirming in her seat. Another gesture that Avery noticed. He cleared his throat. "What should I do?"

"I've got a friend. I'll fix you up. Two weeks from Friday. That should be enough time. We can do dinner."

Avery pulled out his Palm Pilot. "Oh, no can do. Have dinner with the parents Friday evening at The Four Seasons."

Joe swore under his breath, which Amanda ignored, majorly curious at the thought of seeing Joe with his parents. How had he and Avery turned out so absolutely opposite? From what she remembered of the Barringtons, they were just like Avery. Joe had always been the rebel.

"Perfect! We'll all go! Avery, I'll call Penelope." She batted her eyelashes at Avery, a blatant misuse of her feminine wiles. Necessary when engaged in battle. "Let's!"

Avery shared Joe's look of discomfort, but at least he nodded his head. "All right. I trust your taste in all things—" he glanced at Joe "—almost all things, so I'll leave myself in your capable hands. A lump of clay to be molded, so to speak…"

"Good night, Avery," Joe said, standing.

"But I've only just arrived," Avery began.

Joe slipped an arm around Amanda. She leaned back against him, felt a warm kiss against her neck. Her blood heated and her lashes drifted shut.

She melted into her own little pool of nirvana and heard brisk footsteps on the cold marble floor and the sound of the door shutting decisively.

Heaven.

For one long moment, Joe stood behind her, she felt his heart beat against her back, felt the strong muscles in his chest, felt the all-too-real proof of his desire pressing against her thigh.

This was the moment she had waited for.

She turned in his arms, gazed up at his face, and prayed for his kiss. The blue depths of his gaze heated, then burned. Burned for her.

And then, at last, he blinked. He pulled away from her, his look turned cool, impartial.

Damn. She rubbed her arms, feeling a chill in the room for the first time. She looked around the empty apartment, so lifeless, full of white and empty spaces.

Then she stared at Joe. Black jeans, black boots, dark hair. No color at all, yet the apartment seemed full of his light, full of him.

He backed away farther. "Well, I suppose I should go now."

"You don't have to—" Amanda started.

"I owe you an apology," he interrupted.

"For what?"

He shrugged sheepishly. "You tried."

On the other hand, *her* grin was quite triumphant. "You noticed that, hmm?"

"I should have believed you."

"Yes."

"Next time I will."

"Good." She pressed her luck. She wanted him in her apartment, in her life. "Why don't you stay for dinner?"

He shook his head. "I don't think that's a good idea."

"Why? Are you dieting?"

He laughed, his eyes crinkling at the corners. "Do you think I should?"

She studied the fitted shirt that clung to the broad shoulders, highlighting his hard stomach and smooth muscles. No jury would ever convict her if she jumped him right now. She closed her eyes and exhaled. Sanity returned. "You don't need any more compliments, bucko. Your head's already too big."

"But they'd mean more coming from you—" he wheedled. Abruptly he turned away. "I should go."

"I've got fresh pasta, homemade sauce. I can have garlic bread in less than thirty minutes."

That got his attention. He took one step closer. "You really cook?"

"I told you, I'm full of surprises." She picked up the glasses from the coffee table. Adjusted the magazines until the corners were perfectly even. "Stay, Joe."

She met his gaze full on. Her desire was there, unhidden for him to see.

This time, he didn't blink. "All right, I will."

JOE SAT ACROSS from Amanda at the table, eating absolutely some of the best spaghetti he'd ever had. "You're great at this."

"It's my father's recipe."

He stopped, his fork halfway to his mouth. "Your father cooks?"

"Don't all men?"

Dangerous territory. He stuffed his mouth full and nodded, murmuring sounds of assent. He'd never thought about cooking before. Hmmm.

She laughed at him. There wasn't anything mean or vindictive in her laughter, only something warm and...nice.

Maybe he should start cooking. Damn, she was starting to get to him. Maybe Avery had been onto something when he'd fallen for Amanda. Nah. He shook his head, refusing to admit Avery was right about anything.

"What's your favorite thing to eat?" she asked, an innocent question.

He swallowed another mouthful of ambrosia. She had raised cooking to an art form. "Beef Wellington."

Her smile could have been an art form as well. Mysterious, amused, a Mona Lisa look.

"You have your brother's taste in food."

"It's a Barrington thing." He shrugged it off, not wanting to think about similarities between he and Avery. As far as Joe was concerned, there weren't any. "What do you like?"

"Breakfast. Eggs Benedict. Waffles, French Toast." She closed her eyes and inhaled. "And hot fresh-brewed coffee."

Eggs Benedict? He could do that, couldn't he? He took in her exquisite look of pleasure and knew that he'd move heaven and earth in order to be the cause of that hedonistic expression.

For a moment the thought stunned him. Amanda and hedonistic didn't belong in the same sentence. Yet, there she sat, looking like some Greek goddess ready to go splashing around nude in the water. His body responded instantly. *Ka-pow.* He adjusted the napkin on his lap. Just in case.

"You want to be a pilot." A long strand of pasta dangled from her fork and she took it in her mouth, sucking it in like a kid. A dangerous combination of innocence and sexy cunning. Her eyes were wide and guileless, but her words were what mattered.

Forget hedonistic, she was just trying to turn him into something he wasn't. Sophisticated, intelligent, ambitious. He'd heard what Avery had said, and Joe wasn't playing that game.

"Yes." He studied the wine in his glass. "This is pretty good. What it is?"

"Avery brought it. I don't remember." She dabbed at her lips with the linen napkin. "Why?"

"Just curious."

"No, why do you want to be a pilot?"

She wasn't going to let him off easy. He gazed at the dazzling skyline outside the window. All those lights. All those dreams. And noise—the constant heartbeat that powered the city. Even at night it was there.

What about his dreams? He turned back to Amanda, and suddenly dreams and reality got all muddled. "It's the ultimate. Man conquering the heavens. Steering a one hundred ton machine through the belly of the gods." He laughed, embarrassed.

Amanda didn't laugh, she looked serious. "You should do it, then."

Ambition. Uncomfortable with that thought, he rolled his shoulder. "Yeah, well, then there's reality, Amanda. Sometimes the price is too high. Not all of us were meant to be fabulously successful."

"No one's *meant* to do anything. Your life is your own. No one makes it or breaks it for you."

"Yeah, I read that on a fortune cookie once."

An awkward silence filled the room. He'd ticked her off. And maybe part of him did it on purpose. A ticked-off Amanda he could handle.

He watched as she carefully put her napkin down on the table, and then walked across the room. When she stopped in front of the stereo she bent slightly and adjusted the volume.

Every time she moved, he knew. Every time she breathed, he noticed. He wanted to look away, but he couldn't.

"I think Vincent's going to have a case."

Joe shook his head. "Excuse me?"

"I looked through the *Times'* archives. The cleaning solvent manufacturer settled a case out of court. We filed suit against the company this afternoon."

And Joe had thought Avery was amazing. "You've done all that in two days?"

She thumbed through the stack of CDs next to the stereo. "Really four. There's Friday, plus the weekend, and then I got in early this morning."

Just looking at all that energy inside her made him tired. "How early?"

"Doesn't matter. Dessert?" There was an invitation in her eyes, clearly telling him she was willing to share more than a little chocolate. His mouth filled with the memory of her taste. He slowly put his fork down, then placed his napkin on the table.

"Speaking of early, I've got to be up at four." He stood.

"Some other time," she murmured.

He closed his eyes, wondering if he should do it. Could he make love to her, discover all the warmth and heat that lay under the cool exterior? He liked thinking of her as icy. That made her untouchable and safe. The thought of her pale blue eyes swimming with fire terrified him.

The next morning, he'd wake up and he'd have to look in the mirror, with Avery's scent lingering in the air once more.

"You have a screwy sense of honor, Joe."

For a moment he thought his conscience had developed a voice. She looked small and lonely staring out at the city.

His hands clenched. "Better screwy than none, right?"

Nobody laughed.

"You've got this role in your head that you think you have to play, but you've outgrown it."

"No, it's not a role. I just learned to accept who I am. Somebody's always gotta take second place."

"Joe, you're more than that."

His heart twisted. Heart twisting was not good. "Look, the affirmations are nice, but really, I like my life. You don't need to change it for me."

"You could do more," she said quietly.

He thought about laughing, but she might take that wrong. No, he couldn't do more. He'd tried to live up to Avery. That didn't work. And now there was Amanda. "And that's the difference between you and me, isn't it? You're like a fairy-tale princess who locked herself in some ivory tower far away from the real world. I like my world, though. I don't want more."

Amanda whirled around, her gaze fixed on him. She looked like she was ready to cry. Hell. "I'm going to paint my apartment red."

Where did that come from? He looked at the beige walls, and the subtle prints. "Isn't that a little extreme?"

"Red, Joe. Screaming red." Her bottom lip turned up, and she planted her hands on her hips. The pale blue eyes were hot.

He needed to leave. Now. He took a step toward the door. "Red would be good. I need to go."

She followed him. The sound of her sheer stockings sliding over the marble was an oddly intimate sound that he didn't want to hear.

But she wasn't done yet. "You're using Avery as a shield, Joe."

"Maybe I am."

"Is the thought of making love to me so frightening?"

The thought of making love to her was pure bliss. But Amanda carried a high price. *I'd just disappoint you, Amanda. Been there, done that.* "I don't want a relationship" is how he ended up answering her.

"Maybe I don't either."

"You're not that kind of girl," he said, wanting to get out of this conversation quickly. It was getting harder and harder to remember why he had to leave.

"And that's the only kind you ever get involved with, right? I never said I wanted to marry you," she said in a quiet voice.

"No, that'd certainly be a cold day in hell, wouldn't it?" He took hold of the doorknob and twisted.

"Joe," she put a hand on his arm.

He stared deep into her eyes, seeing concern and pity reflected there. The pity is what spurred him on. "What's the matter, Amanda? None of your usual crowd giving you any? You want to get laid?" he said, trying to sound like he wasn't dying inside.

Damn.

He had to get out of there.

"Good-bye Amanda," he said, closing the door behind him. But instead of walking away, he just stood there, staring at the impenetrable barrier separating them.

No. Damn it all, *no.*

"Amanda?"

"Go away, Joe," she said from behind the door.

"I'm sorry. I shouldn't have said that."

"No, you shouldn't have. Go away."

Joe stuffed his hands in his pockets and started down the empty hallway.

Give it up, Barrington.

He spun on his heel and turned back. "Would Eggs Benedict help?"

"What?"

"If I made Eggs Benedict, would it help?"

"No."

He had just pressed the elevator button, when she opened her door. "But you might want to try it anyway."

_____ **7** _____

THE SMOKE ALARM wouldn't shut up. Joe kept dous-
ing the pan with water, the kitchen floor was now
completely wet. What a disaster. The fire was out,
but the cast iron skillet still sizzled and popped. And
then there was the smoke. Lots of smoke.

Bam. Bam. Bam.

The door sounded as if somebody was trying to
break it down. Now what? Joe took one last look at
the complete mess in his kitchen and then ran to
open his door.

He fumbled with the lock, and the pounding
stopped. He flung the door open. Vincent stood
there with a baseball bat.

"You're here!"

Millions of wiseass remarks sprang to Joe's lips,
but he remembered his resolution. *For today, I will
not be a jerk.* "Yeah," he answered.

Vincent charged into the room, brandishing the
bat like a weapon. "I called 9-1-1—"

Sirens blared down the street.

"I've got everything under control," Joe yelled,
like he burned food in his kitchen every day. From

his window, he could see the pride of New York running into his building.

Vincent disappeared into the smoke emanating from the kitchen. The fire alarm screeched in long bursts.

"What were you doing in here?" Vincent hollered. "I haven't seen that much smoke since Manny Abramson cleaned his burners with lighter fluid. Even I can spot the difference between Fantastic and EverLight. I don't know what they're going to do with him. He can't take care of himself much longer." Vincent's voice trailed off, and there was more thudding as the sound of heavy boots pounded on the steps.

The fire department was here.

Joe held up a hand as a team of six firemen appeared at his door. "S'all right this time, guys. Got everything under control." Joe hoped the captain would ignore the blasting alarm.

The captain leaned against his ax. "You're sure, son?"

Joe laughed in what he hoped was a confident manner. "Yup. A little accident in the kitchen."

The fireman looked at him, a question in his eyes.

The alarm stopped. Thank God. Joe owed Vincent for that.

Joe nodded once more.

"Cooking?"

Joe felt a warm flush that had nothing to do with the heat from the kitchen. "Yes, sir."

The fireman's face split into a grin. "You wouldn't believe how many calls we get like this. You single?"

"Yeah."

The captain grew serious. "Well, we need to get a look at the kitchen, but it shouldn't take too long." After a quick but thorough inspection, the captain spoke to Joe. "Be more careful next time, son. One grease fire is all it takes."

"Sorry, sir. I will. I promise."

Joe waved until the men were out of sight and then closed the door, leaving him alone with Vincent, a smoky room and a huge mess. Time to get to work.

Vincent came out of the kitchen with the incriminating evidence. "What was this in its former life?" He held up the blackened frying pan.

Joe sank into his chair. His comfort. He ran a hand through his hair. The pan was history. One day old and it would never see another. There was a reason Joe didn't cook. "Eggs Benedict."

Vincent stared at the pan, then back at Joe, then back at the pan. "You need help."

Well, that was the understatement of the year. He started to laugh, half in fun, half on the verge of serious mental collapse. It'd take more than carbonized Eggs Benedict to dampen his hopes. Joe sucked in some air. The day was still young.

"Yup. And I'm ready to learn."

AMANDA ALLOWED herself to sleep in and woke up the next morning at 5:37 a.m. That was just enough time to wash, dry, curl and dress and still be at work by seven. She had just finished dressing when the bell rang. One of her neighbors? When she opened the door, no one was there, just a small glass dish.

She stared down the hallway. Empty.

Hmmm. She opened the lid and smiled. Eggs Benedict. There was a note attached.

Amanda,

Eggs Benedict, Day One. If you could please leave the container outside the door when you're done. Don't worry about washing it. I'll take care of that. Also, if you could check the appropriate boxes below.

☐Too much cayenne
☐Not enough cayenne
☐Too cold, please heat more next time
☐Temperature just right
☐Sauce too runny
☐Need more sherry
☐Perfect

I wish things were different, Amanda.

See you soon,

Joe

She ate the eggs, marked the "Not enough cayenne" box, just to throw him off, and put the dish outside her door. She wished things were different, too. And if she got her way, they would be.

Amanda,

Eggs Benedict, Day Two. I added more cayenne, but it tasted really hot to me. See what you think. Also, I'm leaving you a cookbook for five-minute meals. You do too much.

☐ Too much cayenne
☐ Still not enough cayenne
☐ Perfect
☐ Still mad at Joe
☐ Not quite as mad at Joe

See you soon,

Joe

Amanda,

Eggs Benedict, Day Three. Okay, I think I've got the eggs down now. Since you're still mad, I made breakfast potatoes as well. They turned out pretty good.

☐ Add cheese
☐ Not enough cayenne (for the potatoes)
☐ Perfect
☐ Still extremely mad at Joe
☐ Still mad at Joe
☐ Potatoes were a step in the right direction

See you soon,

Joe

Amanda

Eggs Benedict and breakfast potatoes, Day Four. Do you think I should add some swiss cheese instead of the cheddar to the potatoes? Or maybe both?

□Want swiss and cheddar
□I hate swiss. Why didn't you know that?
□Ditch the cheddar
□Ditch Joe
□Still mad at Joe
□Only slightly mad at Joe
See you soon,

Joe

Amanda,

Eggs Benedict and Breakfast potatoes, Day Five. I can tell you're softening. The check marks don't look so violent anymore. Glad you're liking the potatoes. I brought some O.J., as well.

□Don't like O.J., please change to apple juice
□Need coffee
□Milk?
□Thinking that Joe might be an okay guy
□Thinking that Joe is an ass.
See you soon,

Joe

"SO, YOU'RE Mary Sunshine today. Looks like somebody is getting some." Grace perched herself on Amanda's desk, attired in an American flag pantsuit.

"Not some. Only breakfast."

"A gentleman friend is making breakfast for you?"

Amanda buffed her nails on her white silk vest.

"Only for the last five days. Eggs Benedict, potatoes, and café mocha." Joe was coming around to her way of thinking; she knew it.

"Oh, that Dr. Barrington, he's something, isn't he?"

"No, no, no. It's Joe Barrington, thank you very much."

"No way, boss!"

"Way." Amanda nodded, quite pleased with herself. "He gave me a cookbook, too." And tonight, she was going to really let loose and make E-Z Chicken Stroganoff.

"Oh, sounds like he's smitten. He really cooks, though? I mean, Lenny Titolo cooked a mean lasagna, but he really raised his brothers and all, and then after he married Mary McAnnally, he just turned into a porker. So, he really cooks?" Grace peered over the rims of her glasses at Amanda.

"Joe cooks quite well."

Grace was impressed. "And if he's good in the kitchen, is he just as good in the boudoir?"

"Grace, that's none of your business."

"He's not, is he? Tsk, tsk. Those good-looking ones are always too confident. Please me, baby, or I'm outta here."

That didn't seem fair to Joe. Amanda defended him. "Actually, I must disagree. What I've seen is outstanding. He does these great long kisses."

"Only kissing?"

"We're going to close the deal real soon or I'm not Amanda Sedgewick."

"Well, you go, girlfriend. I don't know a man alive who can resist a woman with a little hanky-panky on her mind."

That earned a frown from Amanda. There was one. Joe "I'm An Old-Fashion Neanderthal" Barrington. But that was going to change very soon. "I've never really seduced a man before."

Grace peered from behind her frames. "No?"

Amanda bounced her pen on the desk. "Have you ever seduced a guy?"

"Millions of 'em."

"Millions?" Amanda looked at Grace with new eyes.

"Well, four. Maybe five if you count Eddy Delvecchio."

"What works?"

"Aggression. Honey, take no prisoners. You got to look 'em in the eye, and say, 'I want your sex.'" She pouffed her hair. "It's never failed me. Except with Eddy, but he's gay, and I didn't know it until Linda told me, and then I didn't want to believe her, but when he turned me down, and I had on my Lolita skirt, one hundred percent guaranteed satisfaction, I knew it was true."

"What's a Lolita skirt?"

"One of those short, little flouncy things and then you go commando."

Commando? Amanda took a deep breath, taking

note of the panty hose, camisole, and discreet white underwear that she was wearing underneath her dress. She didn't know about going without underwear. That sounded extreme. *And slightly wicked.* She lowered her voice. "And everyone can see?"

"Well, only if they're looking. You remember, Sharon Stone, *Basic Instinct?*"

Maybe there was something to it. "I bet fairy-tale princesses don't go commando, do they?"

"No, a princess is strictly Victoria's Secret. They don't got the goods." Grace stood up, folders in hand. "What'cha thinking, boss?"

Amanda started doodling on the paper in front of her. Skirts with panty-lines and Victoria's Secret undergarments. She sighed and marked a big X right through the middle. "I'm thinking I never liked being holed up in an ivory tower anyway."

ON WEDNESDAY Joe actually dared to pick up the phone and call her. She wanted an affair. He wanted an affair. Neither of them was looking for a serious relationship. Hell, that'd be a joke, wouldn't it?

Still, this was Amanda, and all the lines, all the smooth moves that Joe had ever used, just didn't seem to fit. for the first time in his life, Joe had no idea how to proceed.

Amanda needed romance and candlelight, and Joe wanted to give her that. But how?

All week there'd been dreams. Amanda was on *60 Minutes*, being interviewed, wrapped in nothing but one of her white satin sheets. He kept waiting for the sheet to slip lower, but it never did. She answered every question with poise and confidence. Looking every bit like the superstar she was.

How could a guy live with that?

Joe couldn't, could he? God, but he wanted to. Maybe there was a way after all.

It took a different sort of man than Joe to walk away from that sort of woman. He dialed her number.

THE NEW YORK CITY courtroom was imposing and awe-inspiring. Amanda loved to come here and absorb the scent of hundred-year-old wood overlaid with the smell of justice.

The lawyer for Clean-All Industries was Robert Kendall from Peters and Solomon. Amanda had heard of him, but had never seen him in action. He was one of those high-dollar sharpshooter attorneys. She tapped her pencil against her notes and tried not to smile. Today, she was going up against the big boys, and it was bad form to show your hand too early. Instead, she leaned down under the table and pretended to adjust her shoe, giving in to the urge to grin.

"All rise." Amanda stood, giving Kendall a polite nod. *He was toast.*

Judge McKee was a stickler for starting on time and today he looked particularly impatient as he scurried into the courtroom, robes flying in his wake.

"Okay, let's move this along. It's my anniversary and I'm meeting my wife for lunch. I need to be out of here in," he turned to the clerk, "how much time?"

The shorter lady at his side checked her watch. "Forty-five minutes, your honor."

"Forty-five minutes it is." After the attorneys stated their names and clients for the record, the judge pointed to Amanda. "Ms. Sedgewick, you're up."

Amanda stood up and took one last look at her notes. "Your Honor, Mr. D'Antonio has filed this action against Clean-All Industries alleging claims sounding in negligence and strict liability. In order to prepare this case, it is imperative that we receive the discovery requested, as reflected in Plaintiff's brief and the exhibits and affidavits we've filed with it. The defendants' objections are nothing more than roadblocks thrown in front of my client in an attempt to paper this case and hope that he'll meekly turn tail and run." Amanda shot Kendall a glance. "I assure you, Mr. D'Antoni is here for the long haul." She glanced down to check her notes.

Kendall took advantage of her pause to interrupt. "But Your Honor, any alleged wrongdoing occurred over thirty years ago. Even if Clean-All was liable in this situation, and I'm certainly not saying that, the statute of limitations would long since have expired."

Amanda frowned at Judge McKee, looking as if

she was worried. "You Honor, Mr. Kendall can certainly raise limitations in a motion for summary judgment. But since he hasn't, I suggest that we focus on the motion that's before the court. My client has a right to the documents requested in the request for production. As you can see from the affidavits attached as exhibits A through T, we believe those documents will show that Clean-All was aware of the toxic component of its cleaner. We can prove that awareness through the settlement documents we've requested."

"There was a settlement in this case?" The judge looked concerned.

"Not with my client, Your Honor," Amanda answered. She'd anticipated that question from the bench. "Our investigation has revealed that three of Clean-All's employees entered into a settlement in 1971. As you can see from the affidavits, that settlement resulted from the employees' threat to sue for injuries resulting from breathing toxic fumes."

Kendall interrupted. "Exactly, Your Honor. That was over thirty years ago. Limitations has run."

Amanda stood up straighter. "The discovery rule applies in this case, You Honor."

Kendall took the bait. "Your Honor, the employees Ms. Sedgewick is referring to were obviously aware of the alleged toxicity. There is no reason to believe that Mr. D'Antoni would not have been just as cognizant. The discovery rule doesn't apply."

This was it. Amanda cleared her throat. "It certainly does, Your Honor. Mr. D'Antoni was not in the same position as those plaintiffs. He worked for the airline, not Clean-All. Clean-All deliberately and maliciously failed to inform the airline—or its mechanics—about the dangerous effects of long-term exposure. Those documents that we seek go directly to both this concealment and to the broader question of liability. My client needs those documents not only to establish liability, but to counter any limitation argument that Mr. Kendall may choose to raise."

Amanda turned to Kendall. *Checkmate, my friend.*

"Point taken, Ms. Sedgewick." Judge McKee studied the papers in front of him. Amanda held her breath. All her ducks were in order. Her motion and brief, the requests and responses, the affidavits of the prior plaintiffs and copies of every single case she could find that even remotely addressed the point—all highlighted and tabbed for the judge's easy reference, of course.

Finally, he looked up. "Very good, Ms. Sedgewick. Mr. Kendall, you should have done your homework. Motion to compel is granted. Mr. Kendall, your client has thirty days to turn over the documents that Ms. Sedgewick has requested." The judge turned to the clerk. "How much time?"

The clerk checked her watch. "You still have thirty minutes, Your Honor."

The judge grinned. "Perfect. I'll have time to stop and get some roses."

EDWARD POWERS, the senior partner at Amanda's firm, was waiting at the back of the courtroom. What was he doing here? Witnessing her history-making legal triumph, *that* was what he was doing here. Amanda assumed a professional stance as he approached. "Edward, I didn't realize you were here."

"I had some papers to pick up, Amanda." He held out a hand to her. "Excellent job."

She shook his hand. "Well, it's only the first step. Kendall wasn't bluffing on filing a Motion for Summary Judgment, and his firm's certainly got the wherewithal to bury us in paper. Even once we have documents showing the concealment, the legal briefing on the application of the discovery rule is going to be intense."

"I have the utmost confidence in you, Amanda. You'll be partner before you know it."

Amanda nodded in what she hoped was a wise manner. "I hope I can live up to the high standards of the firm, sir."

"Ambitious lawyers with a strong work ethic is all that we ask."

Amanda smiled cheerfully. "That's me, sir."

Amanda waited until Powers was out of sight before she left the courtroom and took off down the main hall. She was going to be late meeting Joe.

THE METROPOLITAN Museum of Art was the one holdover from Joe's childhood that he enjoyed. His mom had taken him here every Wednesday. It was an old habit, and for meeting Amanda, it was perfect. It was public, a place where they could talk and it was private, so they wouldn't be disturbed.

She looked gorgeous, like normal. She wore a white suit. He was in jeans. It was nearly laughable. They wandered outside first, looking at all the sidewalk artists. Most painted for the tourists, using the New York skyline for subject matter.

There was one he wanted to show her, though. "Come with me." He headed for the last vendor on the street—Martin Kandolfsky, an implant from Moscow.

Joe pointed to a small canvas, a blurring of blue and green, with swirls of white. "Can you figure it out?"

Amanda leaned in close, following the lines with her finger. "It's human, isn't it?"

"It is," the artist replied. "Your untrained eye sees only a fraction of what can actually be contained on canvas. You paint a woman's body and she is nothing more than the collection of her lines, curves, and shadows. You paint her soul, reaching for things she wants to achieve—her dreams, her passions—then, you have great art."

Joe thought he might be right. At only twenty-four, the artist had already attracted a small following.

"So that's a soul, not a face?"

Joe nodded. "Art, like everything else, should go beyond the surface."

INSIDE THE MUSEUM, Joe and Amanda wandered around, finally ending up with the statues.

One marble figure caught her attention. "Andrew Jackson?"

Joe wasn't surprised she had notice. It was good. "Yes."

"In a toga?"

"The artist was going for a look."

"Oh." Amanda looked closer, inspecting it carefully. "It's very realistic, but there's something larger than life about it."

"It's the artist. He wanted everyone he sculpted to be something bigger than they really were. It should be so easy."

She moved to the next statue, a young boy playing on cymbals, and then read the card. "Genius of Mirth."

It was one of Joe's favorites. Joy captured forever. The boy didn't care what he was going to be when he grew up, he was caught in one moment, for a lifetime. "Thomas Crawford."

"You like the sculptures the best?"

He nodded. "Marble is closest to how things really look."

Her eyes studied Joe rather than the piece of art. "They look frozen."

"So's most of the world."

Amanda tilted her head, her look full of questions.

Joe shrugged. "We all have moments where we go

through the motions, just so we can have the times when we're alive."

"When do you feel alive?"

He never should have said anything. "You don't want to know."

"No, it's a serious question."

"You sure?"

"Tell me."

"When I'm around the planes."

"Not when you're around people? I never pegged you for a loner."

He held a finger to his lips. "Sssh. Don't tell anybody." Planes never judged anybody. And that was way too deep for this kind of an afternoon. Time to change the subject. "How's work?"

Amanda began to glow. "Absolutely fabulous."

Her good spirits were contagious. He smiled. "That good, huh?"

She began to pace in front of the statue. "I had to go to court today. Get a motion to compel for Clean-All to release some documents that were used in the prior case. We're going to nail 'em, Joe. They knew exactly what their product was doing to people, and they ignored it."

"You're going to fix it, aren't you?"

"Damn straight." At the moment, she looked like she could rule the world. She looked at her watch. "Speaking of work, I should get back to the office."

Was she that anxious to get rid of him? "You've only been here for ten minutes."

"Yeah. I have loads of stuff to do." She stared up at him, a look that made him nervous and terrified and more than a little glad. "I don't want to go."

That seemed easy enough. "Then don't."

"But then nothing will get done."

"Yes, it will."

"How?"

"You'll get to it eventually." He walked on down the hallway, and she followed. Then he stopped in front of a painting of a storm, a rocky coast and an old clipper ship cruising into disaster. It drew the eye, kept you fascinated, wondering what would happen. He'd have given anything to have that much talent, that sort of skill. "You see this?"

Just as he had done the first time he saw it, she traced it with her eyes. Noting the detail. The color. The passion. "It's beautiful."

"It took the artist eleven years to finish."

Amanda laughed. "I bet it drove him nuts. I've got a two-page to-do list and that's plenty."

"Nah. He just had to finish things in his own way."

She shook her head. "My boss would kill me."

She worked too hard. "How many hours do you work in a week, Amanda?"

"Eighty to a hundred."

She definitely worked too hard. "Haven't you ever played hooky?"

"No, I've never needed to."

That was about to change. "And when's the last time you went to the park?"

Amanda thought for a minute. "I don't remember."

"You do work too much."

"But if I don't do my job, then people who really need my help won't get it."

Trust Amanda to be driven by something more humane than money. He shouldn't have been surprised. "After a while, you'll stop caring. Then what good will you do?"

"I can't just take off." She looked almost embarrassed.

Avery would say he was corrupting her. "Amanda, it's a job. You have a life, too."

"But I've worked so hard."

Avery would be right. "And you've done wonderfully, but is that all you want to do?"

"You think I should quit and weave baskets in Montana?"

"No. But I think there's a lot more inside you than just a career." She should realize that. "Don't you have a hobby?"

"Well, I used to cross-stitch, but then I never could finish, so I gave it up."

He thought. "Do you read?"

"Oh, all the time. I have to keep up with the medical review journals, and then the *Annals of Occupational Hygiene,* and *Ecotoxicology and Environmental*

Safety." She stopped. "That's not what you're talking about, is it?"

Joe made up his mind and grabbed her hand. She needed a white knight more than she knew. "Come on."

HE BOUGHT two hot dogs, one soft drink and a copy of *Harry Potter.* They found a bench outside a quiet spot, and he started to read to her. After two hours, she was enthralled.

"Why did you read this?" she asked. "I never would have picked it up. It's a kid's book."

"I like Harry."

"He's kinda sad."

Joe traced the hardwood bench with his finger. "Yeah, but he's just an average kid."

"Well, no, he's a magical wizard, and for goodness sakes, he's got a lightning bolt on his head."

"Maybe, but I don't think that's the author's point. It all boils down to one average kid trying to make his life mean a little more."

Joe looked so earnest as he talked. Earnest and confused. Amanda reached out for his hand. "It's just a book, Joe."

He looked down at their two hands and laughed. "Yeah. Silly me." When he looked up, his eyes were full of warmth. "I'm glad you're here."

Somewhere in the distance, dogs were barking and kids were laughing. But everything in Amanda was focused on the intensity in his eyes. They weren't talking about *Harry Potter* anymore. "I'm glad you asked."

"Amanda?"

She liked the way his voice dipped when he said her name. "Hmmm?"

"You're nothing like what I thought you'd be."

"How so?"

"You're not so—" he pushed a strand of hair away from her face "—stuffy. I thought you'd be all business, all the time, but you get so fired up when you talk about your work."

In a couple of minutes Joe was going to realize that it wasn't her work that got her fired up. He moved closer and her nose tingled from the musky smell of his cologne. "I'm not all work, Joe."

He traced her lips with a light finger and she shivered. "Not with that mouth, you're not."

"Is that an insult, Mr. Barrington?"

At the same instant she reached up for him, he lowered his head. Great minds. "I would never insult your mouth, Amanda," he murmured against her lips. "Never."

It started quite innocently, soft and teasing, a mere brushing of lips. His tongue traced just inside her mouth, shooting quick sparks of need through her. When she wanted more, he held back.

Today, he seemed to be in no hurry. She loved the flavor of him. It was wonderfully decadent. Joe was a temptation that she could not resist. He didn't hide anything from her. His steady breath, the quickening beat of his heart. The way his hands stroked and pressed. All of it went straight to her head.

Quietly, a breeze settled around them. In the distance, the city moved forward. Cars honking and somewhere in the distance a man was singing. Yet their single bench had become a haven.

Unable to help herself, she took his lower lip in her mouth and sucked, fascinated by the feel of his jaw under her fingertips, the rough stubble that lined it.

Joe pulled her closer, until she sat in his lap, his hands pushing restlessly inside her jacket.

With an easy sigh, she melted into him. Already her body was beginning to throb and heat. Her tongue tangled with his, impatient, but then he slid his tongue deeply in her mouth and covered her heart with his hand, his touch gentle and soothing.

He kissed her with a slow, incessant rhythm that made her shift her hips until she could feel his erection underneath her. Even then, it wasn't enough. She rubbed against him, the friction of his jeans a poor substitute for what her body was demanding.

Nearby voices buzzed in her head, reminding her of where they were. Joe lifted his head, tracing her cheek with an unsteady hand. "You're making me lose it, Amanda."

"You don't look sad."

"No. Not at all." He looked down at his watch. "Look at the time. Three-thirty. You should go. You're not going to finish all that work you have."

He was watching her. This was another test. If it

hadn't been for an important call to Vincent's insurance company, she would have stayed. She wanted to stay. But she did need to finish the prep work for the Fidelity negotiation, and a co-worker's performance on the Northcott case was pretty spotty. If she didn't look over his shoulder, nobody would.

"I can't," she answered, kissing him softly. Amanda stood, brushing out the wrinkles in her suit.

Joe shrugged as if it didn't matter. "No big deal. I'll see you later."

THE NEXT MORNING, Amanda looked up at the clock on the office wall—8:30 a.m. If there was true justice in the world, it should be 5:00 p.m., considering she'd already put in four hours. She took off her glasses and rubbed her eyes. Her pens were lying sideways and her hand reached out to straighten them, but then she shook her head. Nope. Just gonna leave them. A little disorder never hurt anybody.

Maybe she should have slept in this morning, but gee, then she wouldn't have finished the Petersons' letter to National Mutual Insurance, outlined the depositions for the Leonard case, or read a fascinating discussion in the *New England Journal of Medicine* on the increasing rates of asthma in dairy workers. She'd made eighteen copies and distributed it into everyone's mailbox. Quite productive, all in all.

She opened up her e-mail and scanned the listing of messages. There was one marked urgent from Powers. Ah, the morning was getting a little brighter. She leaned back in her chair and wished she could put her feet up on her desk.

With a cocky click of her mouse, she opened it up and read. Yeah, just as she suspected, Van Zandt was needing help with the Northcott mediation. She'd tried to tell Powers earlier, but did he listen? Noooo. Not to junior lawyer Sedgewick. Not until the case was so deep in legal quicksand, they'd be lucky to salvage any sort of settlement for Mr. Northcott. She reread the last line:

> I know you've been working a lot of hours, but could you get with Van Zandt? I'd consider it a personal favor.

Personal favors. She saved the e-mail in her folder named RainyDaysAreHereAgain, and went to see what was up with Van Zandt.

When Amanda entered Steve Van Zandt's office, he looked up from his computer. "Hey there." He smiled.

Amanda got right to the point. "Powers said you needed help."

The smile dwindled. "Nah, I can handle it."

Hmmm. She shook her head. "When's the mediation?"

"Two weeks."

"Who's the mediator?"

"Lindstrom."

He looked pleased. It was a nightmare. "Have you

read his opinions for *Flanagan v. Rockefeller Medical?* Judge Lindstrom presided over that case when he was still on the bench."

"Uh, no... When was that?"

"Look, you handle the motion to compel and I'll take care of Judge Lindstrom." It'd be a couple of extra late nights, but they could salvage this.

Van Zandt pushed his keyboard away and stood up. "I'm sorry."

Amanda froze. "What for?"

"I should have gotten help earlier. Just found out my wife is pregnant, and well, we've been excited and I've taken some time off. It's hard to work when your mind is elsewhere."

She took a chair, amazed. She didn't even know he was married. "Congratulations."

His smile was truly joyous. "Thanks. It's going to be a girl. Alexandra Michelle."

"How do you do it?" Amanda had always just worked. It was a simple solution.

"You have to make it work, so you do. I'm going to cut back some. Take some easier cases. Wait until you have a husband or a family, then you'll understand. You ever think about getting married?"

Not until recently. It had never seemed appealing before. "Some."

Steve laughed. "You're up for partner in a few months. Wait. Just you wait."

She didn't need to be thinking like that. Time to change the subject. "Why don't you give me the files for the case? I'll take a look. And if you need me, just ask."

"Thanks. I owe you one."

"No, you don't. This one's on the house." Amanda took the files and walked out of the room.

She shut the door behind her and ran straight into Powers.

Amanda juggled the files in her hand. "Good morning, sir."

"Assisting Van Zandt?"

"Yes, sir, but I don't think he needs much help, sir. He's doing a fine job."

"Good, good. Like to hear that. Well, carry on," he said, then he hurried down the hall.

Soon. She had five years under her belt and already they were dangling the carrot in front of her. *Someday soon.*

When she returned to her office she shut her door, then noticed a letter on her desk. Heavy stationary with gold printing no less.

She stared at the letter for a few moments before she opened it.

Dear Amanda,

Although a thank-you note seems out of place, I did want to set your mind at ease. I suppose it is time I move on with my life, but I need to thank you for giving me so much joy. You were kind to me when others weren't, and dreamer that I am, I could conjure up Romeo and Juliet, where instead was only Falstaff and Cinderella.

You always were the consummate lady. Perhaps your only flaw was in being too much the lady, trying not to deflate my sensitive ego. Please forgive my persistence in the past. I seem to play the fool better than most.

I'll say nothing more about my brother. You know my opinion on that subject. You are a pearl and he is Lothario reincarnated and back with a vengeance. Although perhaps I should credit him with some bit of shining armor that you seem to see in him.

I am looking forward to meeting your friend, and will watch my brother carefully. I do not want to see you hurt. If he does, he shall answer to me.

Sincerely,

Avery

Amanda dug in her desk for a box of tissues. Beneath that pompous exterior was a melted marshmallow. She needed to call and tell Penelope how lucky she was. Friday she would be going on a dream date with a marvelous guy—Dr. Avery Barrington, III.

All her life people had made assumptions about Amanda. Now she found herself guilty of the very same crime. The phone lingered right under her fingers. She should call Joe and tell him. This time there was no doubt. The plan was working. Surprise. Not only was Avery getting on with his life, but she was, too.

Now she had a life outside of work. She'd been to the park, a museum, a club, and she had started reading—for fun, even—and she had found the time to talk to her Mom on the phone.

But the biggest surprise of all, she was working fewer hours. Down by about five point seven hours per week, but still...it was a start. And she'd get better.

All because of Joe.

That made her smile. She leaned back in her chair and this time she did put her feet up on the desk—after all, the door was shut. She remembered their conversations, the way he looked at her with those magical eyes of his. All life and heat, and oh...she shivered.

Her fingers lightly touched the buttons on her phone. Maybe he'd just want to see her again because he liked her company. Because she could make him laugh. Because he wanted to kiss her. *Because he wanted to do more...*

She loved the way he kissed, so unrestrained, uncontrolled. Joe knew who he was, and when he kissed you, you knew it, too. And when he took her to bed...

Her eyes drifted shut. The men she'd dated in the past had never even kicked up a sweat in bed. Joe would be different.

He would carry her into the bedroom.... Nah, that was all wrong. They'd barely get the door shut and he'd press her against the wall. Yeah, that was Joe. He'd kiss her then. Muscles holding her against the wall, tongue thrusting inside her mouth, circling. Hungry and greedy. He'd be breathing heavily in her ear, telling her what he wanted to do to her. How she would scream.

Amanda clenched her fists a few times, taking deep breaths. Oh, this was getting good.

He would rip off her shirt, the buttons flying across the room. Her bra would be no obstacle, he'd unfasten the clasp with one hand. His desire had him whipped in a frenzy.

His desire for her. Every bit of her was throbbing, pleading for his hands, his mouth. Her nipples were hard and sensitive, aching to be touched. He'd tell her how perfect she was. Then his lips would clamp over her breast.

At last.

Sucking hard and fast. She would bury her hands in his hair, welcoming the pressure. But she wanted more. She rubbed against him, feeling his erection, the friction between them making her insane.

His hands would fumble at her skirt, and he'd rip his fingers through her hose. She whimpered, wanting relief. He would hold her hard against himself with his big strong hands.

Oh, it was magic, pure magic. His fingers would

plunge inside her. Exploring. Discovering the exact spot that would make her beg.

She'd fumble with his fly, desperate now, almost crying to have him inside her. Wet and hungry for him. He'd laugh and tell her how hot she was. How good they would be together. She moaned weakly, anticipating. And now, just when she was ready to blow, he'd slow everything down to a torturous pace.

His fingers would play inside her, first two, and then three. Everything inside was building, centered on that heated flesh, damp between her thighs. He'd tell her how he wanted to make love to her all night.

She closed her eyes and whimpered.

All night?

Her eyes flew open and she dragged some papers across the desk. Teasing. She'd work her way inside his pants, touching him carefully at first. He'd be all silky and all hard, his breathing shallow. She'd stroke the tip of him, and then he'd moan, and so she'd get serious. He'd jerk up her chin, and their eyes would lock. Slowly she'd stroke him. Then faster.

She smiled to herself. This time, he would beg.

Finally, his pants would go. And then his...boxers or briefs? For Joe? Briefs, definitely briefs.

She could make some lawyer joke. Nah, that would spoil the moment, and she so, so, so badly wanted to get that powerful piece of him inside her. He'd pull her up until she was straddling him, her legs wrapped around his waist. And then, with one blessed thrust, wham, right inside her.

Oh.

He'd start to move and she'd hold on for dear life. He was ravishing her. Her back was pressed against the door, and each time he thrust, she would rap against the door.

The pencil pounded on her desk.

Bam.

Bam.

Bam.

Wait a minute...

Bam!

Bam!

Bam!

Her eyes flew open. "Amanda?" A voice called from the other side of her door.

Powers! Please, no.

Her legs flew down from the desk and she straightened her skirt. Oh, goodness. She pressed her thighs together, her muscles still a little jumpy. "Come on in."

He entered her office and sat down in the chair opposite her desk. That meant he was going to stay.

Darn.

"Amanda, I'd like to thank you for your help with Van Zandt. You've been a real asset lately, picking up whatever needs to be done, finding cases on your own."

"Did you need something, sir?"

"Yes. I have one more favor to ask. An old friend of the family is having some problems with his insurance company and I promised I'd help. I need someone good. I think you're the perfect candidate."

She stared at the pens, so upright and straight. Right in their place. This was it. This was the chance she needed. Help out an old family friend—fast-track to partner. She'd be the youngest one to make it at the firm.

"I'd be delighted to," she started to say, and then stopped herself. "But you know, I don't think I could give the client the attention that he deserves. D'Antoni's case is going to be a real bear and with my existing caseload... The nice thing about Brown, Powers and McGlynn is that all the lawyers are top-notch and you can be sure your friend will get only the very best. You've done a great job assembling talent at this firm, sir. You should be proud." Amanda took one of the pens from the holder and spun it sideways on her desk blotter. She waited, anxious to see his reaction.

His face fell. Disappointment. Darn. "I'm sorry to hear that, Amanda. I knew you were the one." He rose and adjusted his jacket, and then started walking toward the door. And there was her partnership. Walking right out with him.

"Wait!"

He turned, raised a brow. "Yes?"

Amanda walked from behind the desk. She wasn't ready to give it up yet. "If my schedule eases up, if we get a quick recovery from Clean-All, I could take it one."

"But you can't right now?"

She wavered, but in the end she knew her answer. "Well, no."

"I see." Disappointment was back.

Well, that was too bad. Amanda stood her ground. "No, I can't right now. I'm sorry."

He walked out the door and she collapsed in her chair.

What had she done?

8

AMANDA ARRANGED to meet Joe after work—five-thirty at Bow Bridge in the park. She tried to slip out at four-fifty-five without anyone noticing, but as luck would have it, Powers had decided to refill his coffee just when she was slinking down the hall, briefcase and keys in hand. "Out for the rest of day?" he asked, pouring a little sugar in his cup.

She could furnish all sorts of excuses, needing to meet with a client or just wanting to work at home. Any of the standard replies that a partner-in-waiting would make.

"Yes," she said, waiting to see what token alibi she could come up with. But instead of the dedicated, ambitious, nose-to-the-grindstone person she was, she was struck dumb.

"I suppose you know the partners will be meeting next week? Going to see who's naughty or nice. It's no secret you're up for consideration."

"Is it that time of year?" she asked, knowing that the date had been marked on her calendar for several months.

"Yes, you've been working so hard. Doing so well. You have a bright future at here."

"Yes, sir," she said, discreetly checking her watch. She needed to get out of here.

"Are there any new developments in the Northcott case? Has Van Zandt messed it up too badly?"

"Oh, no, no, no. He's got everything taken care of. Nothing much for me to do really. I set up a lunch with the insurance company next week. I think they're ready to start talking about a recovery."

"Good, good." He leaned his hip against the counter. "I knew you were just the person to take on that challenge."

"Anytime, sir." *Just not in the next two hours.*

"And I'm going to keep you in mind. I wanted to talk to you about the D'Antoni lawsuit."

"Yes, yes," she nodded obediently.

"I'm not sure he's got much of a case, Sedgewick. Are you sure there's any potential for recovery there? It's taking up a lot of your time. Without punitives, is it really worth it to us?"

She assumed her authoritative stance, looking Powers right in the eye. "Don't worry. I'm thinking that once we show the other side the memos I found from their old vice president, punitive damages won't be a problem. And Clean-All will be more than ready to talk settlement rather than risk getting slammed by a jury. Punitives will be the least of their worries. They'll be clamoring for a confidentiality agreement to keep the news media off their back. And we'll give it to them, too. For a price."

"I'll defer to your judgment."

She sneaked a look at her watch—five-fifteen. She was going to be late. "I won't disappoint you, sir. Now, if you'll excuse me?"

Powers looked contrite. "I've been keeping you, haven't I? Go on."

"You're sure?" she tried to look sincere.

"Take advantage of it while you can. After you make partner, these warm summer days will be a thing of the past."

Amanda took off down the hall, and as soon as she got out the door, she ran.

JOE CHECKED his watch. She was late. Joe had never considered himself a punctual person, and it had never bothered him before to be kept waiting. But damnit, he'd been counting the minutes all day, and some little part of him had hoped she'd been counting as well. Wrong again, Barrington.

When summer was winding down, Central Park was always busy at six o'clock. There were mothers with toddlers, roller-skating businessmen, and the usual assortment of kids on scooters.

A collie bounded by with a Frisbee in its mouth and its owner in hot pursuit. For a few moments he watched the park, and then he saw her.

She walked with such an easy grace. Her hair swaying around the shoulders when the wind caught it. Heads turned when Amanda walked by, but she was always too busy to notice. He looked down at his own casual dress and frowned. He should have dressed up more. She was dressed in gray pinstripes and it should have looked manly, but jeez, the fitted material did nothing to hide her curves.

Okay, so maybe the day was improving. Radically. Damn, he was lucky. That blonde—that gorgeous, intelligent blonde—was heading right for him.

"Hello, handsome."

"You're late." Not the "I've got to make love to you or die" that he wanted to say, but close enough.

"Do I get a kiss?"

She didn't need to ask, his hands were already reaching out. Amanda leaned in, fitting his body perfectly. At the first touch of her lips, heat seared through him, stealing his breath. God, he could never get enough of her.

He fisted his hand in her shirt, pulling her closer, positioning her between his thighs. She rocked up against him, and he heard someone moan. That someone was him.

How could someone who looked so delicate, so fragile, kiss like that? He needed to breathe, draw some sort of oxygen into his lungs, but he couldn't move. He could stand here for days like this, just feasting on her mouth.

She tore her lips away and buried her face in his neck. He could feel her heart racing against his chest. Maybe it was his own. "Are you doing this deliberately?"

"Doing what?" he managed, when his brain resumed rational thought.

"First the museum, now here." She raised her head. "Always in public. Never private. Why?"

Because she was different. She was the Ritz and champagne, and he didn't trust himself to be alone with her, not until the time was right. He took her hand, noticing how small and pale it looked in his own. She kept her nails painted. An impeccable pearl-pink. He dropped her hand and shrugged. "I hadn't noticed."

She didn't buy it for a minute. "The truth."

This time he looked at her, really looked. "Amanda, what do you want?"

"I told you, the truth."

"No. I mean, what do you want this to be? A fling? Something more?"

When she stared up at him like that, all starry-eyed and full of ideas, he got scared. Part of him wanted to sit her down and say, "I'm not your man." But he held his tongue, waiting, trying not to anticipate her answer.

"I got a letter from Avery today. Mission accomplished. He's giving up on me."

The words frightened him. There were no more excuses anymore. Now everything was real. "What do you want?" He repeated his question, needing her answer more than anything now.

"For the past couple of months, I was thinking just a fling. You always seemed so...unconstrained." Her blue gaze locked with his. "I wanted that."

"Is that what you want now?" If she said yes, he would walk away. There were women he could take. A few hours of mutual satisfaction before he'd get dressed and leave in the middle of the night. But not Amanda.

"No. I want to see where this goes. You can change me, Joe, and that's what I want."

Change? She wanted to change something? "Why the hell do you want to change? You're perfect."

Amanda laughed. "No, I'm not. I don't have a life outside work and I can never relax. I stay up late at night and I don't watch old movies or raunchy cable shows. No, I study case law and read about malpractice."

He took her hand, perfect nails and all. "I thought you loved being a lawyer. Going to be on *60 Minutes*, change the world. Remember that?"

"I don't know. Right now I don't want to think about work. I don't want to think about anything. What about you? I told you what I was thinking. Now it's your turn."

"We don't have to do that."

"Yes, we do," she answered, using her lawyer-voice.

Resigned to his fate, he sighed. "What do you want to know?"

"An affair? More?"

He couldn't believe how completely calm she was, while his palms were starting to sweat. Still, she had been honest. God only knows why, but she wanted a relationship with him. There were expectations with a roll in bed, but he knew he could handle that. But the expectations from a relationship scared him. Responsibility, ambition.

This time, he wouldn't fail. "More," he answered quietly.

"Where to from here?"

To bed, straight to bed. Her smile was flirty, her eyes giving him all sorts of ideas. No, he had a plan for her. Romance, seduction. He wanted their first time to be unforgettable.

"We take things slow. I want everything to be perfect for you."

"What could be more perfect than today? Look at the sun, the flowers. I don't want slow."

He cleared his throat, banishing all sorts of visuals in his head. "Amanda—"

She interrupted before he could finish. "You don't understand. When I said unconstrained, I meant unconstrained. Spur of the moment, spontaneous, live life to its fullest and all that."

Joe stared, trying to make up his mind. It was tempting, *she* was tempting. Finally, he decided. "Unconstrained, huh?" He kinda liked that image. he tugged at her hand. "Walk with me."

"What?"

They walked to the Shakespeare's Garden. It was quiet and out of the way. A few couples lingered on the edges, but he made his way deeper into the garden, where the tall grass and shrubs shut out the rest of the world. This would be perfect. Roses bloomed everywhere and a wooden fence appeared and disappeared between the trees.

He leaned back against the fence. "What do you see?"

"Shrubs. Flowers. Trees," she replied.

This time he pulled her against him, his hands spanning her waist, keeping her close. "Now. Close your eyes. What do you smell?"

She sniffed. "Your skin. The grass. New York."

He pressed a kiss against her neck. Trailed his lips over her ear, let his tongue explore her softness. It was with great satisfaction that he heard her long sigh. "What do you hear?"

"Your breathing. The wind. Whispers."

"That's a long way away, Amanda. Nobody's here." He turned her in his arms and began to work the buttons on her blouse.

"What are you doing?"

"I thought you liked unconstrained? I'm trying to help."

Her eyes flew open, full of shock. "Joe!"

He used his fingertips to close her eyes, watching the pale lashes flutter on her cheeks. A flush colored her cheeks, rose under marble. "Nobody's here. Nobody can see."

He pushed the silken material aside, his hands undoing the clasp between her breasts. "You have such beautiful breasts, Amanda. Absolutely perfect." She felt his rough fingers touch her hard nipples, his thumbs brushing against them softly. "It's the wind, Amanda."

She kept her eyes tightly shut, her thighs clenching together. Already she felt herself throbbing and swollen.

His mouth closed over one of her breasts and pulled. "You taste like honey," he murmured. His strong hands kept her in place, hands that she had longed to feel all over. A sharp breeze blew across her bare flesh and she shivered. Hot and then cold.

"Oh, please." She kneaded the hard strength of his arms with her fingers, but it didn't help.

"Please, what? What do you feel, Amanda?"

"I'm gonna die."

His knees parted her legs, and she felt the hard length of him pressing against her thigh. In the distance she heard voices. She wanted to cry out, tell him to stop, but then his mouth closed over her other breast, his tongue circling her nipple, sending warm tides of pressure between her legs.

"What are you thinking about, Amanda?" he asked, his voice seductive, taunting. He licked a drop of sweat that collected between her breasts. "Are you afraid they'll see you? You shouldn't be afraid."

Her legs were starting to shake, her blood pumping there like a heavy pulse.

The voices grew louder.

"We have to stop," she said, even while she was pulling him closer.

His hands tangled in her skirt, cupping her bottom. "What do you want?"

"I want you, Joe. Now. Please." There was the sound of footsteps getting louder, then just as quickly, they grew softer, more distant.

"Here, in the park?" His laugh was wicked. "But that's so...unrestrained."

She wanted to scream at him. Anything, anything to relieve the urgent ache between her thighs. Tight with frustration, she curled her hips up to his erection and ground against him—hard. It was with a high level of satisfaction that she heard his indrawn gasp. "Now."

Her pager went off. In the quiet, amidst only the strained sound of her breathing, was the blasted chirping that she was ready to condemn to the bowels of telecommunications hell.

He lifted his head and stared at her. His blue eyes were filled with fire. With a trembling hand, she searched in her purse for the blasted device. She took a long look at the number flashing there. Powers.

She tossed the pager up and down like a baseball, eyeing the bushes, thinking how good it would feel to hurl the thing right over midfield. But the damned numbers kept flashing and finally she couldn't stand it anymore.

By the time she'd made up her mind, Joe's eyes had cooled, though the teasing gleam was still there.

He pressed one last kiss against her breasts and then fastened the clasp. Quite deliberately he buttoned her blouse, the light touches sweet torture against her oversensitized nipples.

"Joe..."

He waved a hand. "Like I said. Don't worry about it. I'll see you soon."

She straightened her blouse, and her skirt, making her heartbeat slow to a manageable rhythm. No big deal. Right? When she finally got herself together, she searched the path for him, but it was too late. Joe had already disappeared.

9

THEY WREE SUPPOSED to go out on Tuesday. At the last minute, Joe cancelled. He had to work. They tried to meet at a bar on Wednesday, but he got called in for something from his boss. Amanda didn't want to believe he had an ulterior motive for not seeing her. When Friday rolled around, Amanda stared at the office phone all day, half expecting Joe to cancel the dinner with his parents as well.

Over lunch, she pored over old Clean-All memos and called Penelope, just to confirm.

Amanda had arranged for Penelope to meet Avery at the Barringtons' house and then they'd all leave from there.

Just when full-blown panic emerged, late Friday afternoon, he called from the airport. He would pick her up at her apartment and they would go to his parents' house. Apparently Joe stood by his commitments.

The subway ride was quiet, filled with commuters leaving the city at the end of the day. She didn't say much, didn't see the point. Apparently Joe didn't either. But he watched her.

He was wearing a tie today. *A tie.* Even in a jacket

and slacks, he looked rough and untamed. She noticed several of the ladies looking at him, but he didn't seem to notice. Or maybe he was used to it.

She grabbed a pole as the car squealed to a halt.

"Bayside. Watch the door, please."

Joe held out a hand. Tonight he was the gentleman. She held tight, lingering as long as she could get away with. She loved his hands, loved their strength and hardness.

When they got outside the station, the air cleared, and a breeze ruffled her hair. The Barringtons lived a few miles from where she lived when she was growing up. They rounded a corner and he pointed to a well-maintained colonial with a rose garden beneath the bay window.

"This is it," he said, looking a little pale.

Her palms started to sweat, but she didn't have any reason to be nervous. So she was meeting Joe's parents. Big deal. Would they remember her? She'd only met Mr. Barrington once when he had driven her and Avery to a junior varsity football game. St. Albans was a long time long ago.

Before he rang the bell, Joe straightened his tie, and took a deep breath. Fascinated, she watched him. He was really nervous about this.

Why?

When the door was opened by a tiny woman with a loud voice, Amanda understood. "Joseph Matthias Barrington, as I live and breathe." Phyllis Barrington. She swept him into a mother's hug.

She stepped back and gave Amanda the once-over. "So..." she murmured, and then took Amanda by the arm, leading her inside the house.

The Barringtons' place was actually quite homey, with lace doilies here and there that probably belonged to generations of prior Barringtons. The wall over near the fireplace was covered with family pictures. Sensing an opportunity to do some serious snooping, Amanda took a look. There was Avery with his dad at high school graduation, Avery throwing his cap into the air, Avery in a doctor's coat, Avery holding up a fifteen-pound bass, presumably the same one that was stuffed—did they really stuff fish?—and mounted over the bar. And there was more. But not one of Joe.

Mrs. Barrington sidled forward. "Amanda, you must call me Phyllis. Avery's told us so much about you. And you practice law. Imagine! A real barrister. Of course, Avery's uncle Herbert was a lawyer, too, you know."

She tapped Amanda on the arm. "Oh, listen to me. Avery senior just tells me to put a plug in it, but after thirty-eight years of marriage, I don't listen to him. Just find my *restful qi*."

Her *qi*? Amanda shot Joe a "help-me" glance, but Joe was carefully studying the old upright piano, strategically ignoring his mom.

"It's about time we finally met, seeing as how Avery feels about you."

"She's my date, Mom. Not Avery's. We've been

seeing each other for a while, now." Joe came over and threaded his fingers with Amanda's.

She looked at him, wondering what he was doing. Was this a pretence of a pretence? He smiled at her, but it was strained. Obviously going home wasn't easy for Joe.

She rubbed her thumb lightly over his, a comforting gesture more than a come-on. He squeezed her hand in response.

Not really knowing what else to do, Amanda smiled brightly. "That's right."

"Oh." Mrs. Barrington looked away. "Oh." And her smile faded some. "Would you like to see my artwork? I've got a gallery in the next room."

Amanda noticed one painting, then another on every wall. "You paint?"

"Sculpt, actually. Marble. It's so much closer to reality. Do you like sculpture?"

Amanda smiled as the last piece of the puzzle slipped into place. "Well, Joe's been teaching me—"

The doorbell rang and Joe coughed loudly. "Better get that, Mom."

While Phyllis went to the door, Amanda tempted fate and reached up and kissed Joe on the lips. Just once. Lightly, warmly. He looked at her, surprised.

"That's a mercy kiss, isn't it?"

"Why Joseph Matthias Barrington," she murmured, and then kissed him again. "*That* was a mercy kiss."

He looked ready to say something, but then

Avery, his mother and Penelope walked into the room. Whatever he had been ready to say, it'd have to wait.

Penelope turned heads with her dark looks and perfectly polished veneer. She wore black as a rule, with Jimmy Choo pumps. Amanda didn't do black very often, it tended to make her look washed-out. However, on Penelope it was sophisticated and chic.

Avery took charge, impeccable in a dark suit that seemed just right for him. "Mother, I see you met Amanda. Joe, may I introduce Ms. Penelope Farnsworth."

Penelope looked from Avery to Joe, back and forth, like a dieter let loose at Ben & Jerry's. "You have an amazing set of offspring, Mrs. Barrington."

Phyllis looked at her boys and blushed. "Thank you, Penelope."

Avery rubbed his hands together, pleased as always. Amanda noticed he seemed quite taken with Penelope, which was one small step on the way to an Avery-free life. Mentally she cheered.

"Well, should we all depart?" Avery asked. "I hired a car service for the evening. It'd be quite snug in the BMW."

Penelope nearly swooned.

Phyllis positively glowed. "We just love riding in the limo. Our Avery, he does so much."

Joe looked at Amanda. "You ready?"

She grabbed his arm for support. "Sure."

WHEN THEY ARRIVED at the Four Seasons, Joe saw his father waiting for them in the lobby of the restaurant.

"Son." He clasped Avery's hand in a manly ritual of affection.

Joe spared him and simply waved. "Dad."

His dad smiled back. They all understood each other.

Avery Senior turned to Amanda and held her at arm's length. Phyllis's brows rose in warning, but he ignored her. "And this is Amanda. My, how you've grown!" He smiled at Avery, full of masculine pride.

Amanda, new to the Barrington family eccentricities, stepped back and took Joe's hand. "If it hadn't been for Avery, I'd have never met Joe."

And then she kissed him.

On the lips.

That made three times tonight. Joe was counting. At that moment, he didn't want his father there, or his mother, or Avery, or Ms. Penelope Farnsworth. Right now he wanted to be alone with Amanda. He wanted nothing more than to pull her into his arms and forget about everybody else.

Giving in to temptation, he kissed her back. Longer. With feeling.

Someone coughed, and the maître d' murmured a low, "Good evening, Dr. Barrington." Joe looked around and discovered that once again he'd embarrassed the family. He stared back at Amanda and shrugged.

Too bad.

They proceeded into the restaurant and were seated at a large round table in the center of the room.

Avery monopolized Penelope in conversation, and Amanda, well, Amanda was just watching him with pale, blue eyes. Tonight they were definitely hot. And for the first time tonight Joe found himself looking forward to dinner. He didn't know if it was the tight red dress she was wearing, or something else, but she was smoldering, and in the best possible way.

He just wanted to drown in those eyes. The wait-staff came and went, bringing wine and appetizers. Avery had handpicked the menu for them this evening and everyone seemed to be too busy talking, discussing the food.

"He's doing very well this evening," Amanda said, tilting her head in Avery's direction.

"Yeah."

"It looks like he wants her."

"Yeah." He studied his brother, noted the way his eyes never left Penelope. Avery was never that centered on another person, except at work.

Amanda heaved a sigh, the red material of her dress lifting nicely. "Avery's not the only one. I know what I want now."

"And what's that?"

"Why don't you take me home and I'll show you?"

Joe closed his eyes, picturing Amanda wrapped in

white satin sheets, her hair streaming down her shoulders. He pictured her in his arms, watching her face as he moved inside her.

Would anybody notice if they left right now? He checked his watch. Three more hours.

Her dress caught his attention again. It wasn't her style at all. He'd almost said something, but then stopped himself. Was she doing all this for him? Because that's what she thought he'd like?

He lifted the bottle of cabernet. "Wine?"

Instead of answering, she took a fork and studied the feast in front of them. "Do you like oysters?"

"Yeah, they're okay."

She loaded an oyster on her finger, and raised it to his mouth. "Try this."

He stared at the soft white meat, but knew he was hungry for more than seafood. He closed his lips over her fingers, his tongue lapping at the soft meat, slow and methodical. With a heavy-lidded gaze, he watched her, noting the way the pulse at her throat was pounding.

He was almost painfully hard, really liking the idea of leaving. His parents were totally preoccupied, laughing and chatting with Penelope and Avery. Nothing strange about that. Tonight he didn't mind, though. He turned his attention back to Amanda.

His hand slid under the table, flirting with her thigh. He walked his fingers upward, letting her see exactly what he intended. She was biting her lip, her eyes half-closed. And then her knee bumped against the table, and the silverware went clanking. She jerked her leg away, blushing.

And then the next course arrived.

He tried to eat, but his gaze kept drifting back to her. His hand would stray near hers, an accidental touch. Maybe their thighs brushed up against each other, but each time he'd pull back. Patience, Barrington. Patience.

"Joseph, how are those planes doing?" his father asked, jerking Joe out of his fog.

"Good," he answered.

"What planes?" Penelope asked, wiping her mouth daintily.

"Joe works for the airlines."

"Oh, are you a pilot? I think that's just so cool..."

Avery Senior coughed. "Ah, no, Joe's a mechanic, but we're proud of you, son." He winked.

Joe wanted to slide under the table.

Instead, Amanda picked up his hand and traced her fingers against his palm. "You know, when you fly, you trust yourself to these hands. You trust that when he checks the instrument landing system, everything will be okay. When he inspects the turbine rotor discs, you know the engine isn't going to shut down in midair, or when the oil pressure isn't just right, you know he'll ground an airplane rather than risk a problem. When you board a plane, there are a lot of people who work together to make sure that *you* walk off in one piece. Nobody ever thinks about that, do they? But that's what Joe does."

His jaw dropped. Good thing he had no food in his mouth, because he would have sent it across the table. Where the hell had she learned all that? She looked at him and smiled, that confident, lawyerly, "I'm going to be on *60 Minutes*" smile, and he felt something pulling at his heart.

That something was Amanda.

10

THEY ALL WENT ballroom dancing at Some Enchanted Evening on 57th. It was an old-fashioned place that his Mom and Dad frequented on their anniversary. There were round tables circling the dance floor and a full band played old music from the 1930s and '40s. Far above them, a disco ball shot stars on the ceiling. If he'd been there with anybody else, Joe would have spent the evening cracking jokes about how lame it was.

Tonight he wasn't in the mood for jokes.

One and one-half hours left on his date with Amanda. One and a half hours before he saw Cinderella safely home.

She was an excellent dancer—no surprise there. The way he figured, she did everything well. He swirled her around to the tune of some forgotten love song and pulled her in closer.

She snuggled against him. "I'm thinking you're a really good actor."

He smiled. "And I'm thinking you're a really good wiseass."

"What's Avery doing?"

"Boring Penelope with his life story."

"Really?" Her head jerked toward the small table, where Avery and Penelope appeared to be having a marvelous chat. "It's working, Joe. I told you."

He humored her. "Yeah. Maybe you were right."

"Of course I was right. You'd be surprised about how many things I'm right about. Like us, for instance. Admit it, Joe. We're good together."

He kissed her, long and lingering, his fingers grazing over the curve of her shoulder.

His possessive gaze trailed over her, noting the designer outfit, the discreet line of pearls at her throat and her ears, the pinned-up hair, twisted and poufed. There were dreams and then there was reality.

Each time he looked at his parents, his mother waved at him, as if he'd never grown up. Well, she was wrong and soon he would prove it. As if on cue, his cell phone rang.

He walked Amanda off the floor and answered. "Yes?"

"Joe, Buzz here. You wanted some extra hours, right?"

"Yeah."

"We could use you here tonight. Got a few 'B' checks left over in the hangar. If you're interested?"

"I'll be right there." Joe hung up and put the phone back in his pocket.

"You have a cell phone?" The way Amanda stared, he might have had two noses instead.

"Doesn't everybody?" He kissed her quickly.

"Listen, I need to leave. Come on outside, and we'll take a cab home."

"Leave?"

"Yeah. Work."

"Work?" she repeated with a hitch in her voice, that had nothing to do with affection and everything to do with anger.

Of all the people in the world, he'd figured Amanda would be the one to understand this. While watching her mouth tighten with fury, he realized he'd figured wrong.

"Are you doing this on purpose?"

"What?"

"Work. Is this to teach me a lesson?"

Joe rubbed his eyes, trying to soothe the power-drill that was humming in his head. It didn't help. "What are you talking about?"

"Why are you working so much?"

And it was about time she noticed. "Maybe it's time I grew up. Look at you, look at what you've done. I've been telling myself that I was happy where I was, that I didn't want anymore. Maybe I was wrong."

Amanda went quiet. "Are you sure you're all right?"

"Never better." He kissed her once, and then again.

When she looked up at him, this time he saw uncertainty reflected in her eyes. "I need to see you, Joe. Alone. This waiting is driving me crazy."

She thought *she* was going crazy? Joe's hard-on was becoming a permanent fixture in his life. But he wanted their first time to be special. Something elegant, fancy. Something she'd remember for a long, long time. She walked with him out the door. "Soon, honey. Soon. I promise."

Amanda held his arm. "Stay, just a little bit longer."

"Can't. Look, I've got a few hours off on Saturday. I'll call you and we'll do something then."

"Have sex?"

Just for that, he kissed her again. "Amanda. I'm shocked." He tried to keep his tone light, but if he sounded like he was completely turned-on, well, there it was.

Her cool blue eyes flashed at him. Damn, she looked good when she was angry. "I don't want you shocked, I want you aroused."

Like lightning, he had her pressed against the wall. Locked together from breasts to thighs, he made sure she felt every tortured inch of him. "You don't think I want you? You think I've been killing myself to keep from touching you—" he laughed "— God, I can't even do that right."

"You must be joking," she said, sounding completely rational.

Her calm attitude did it. He didn't answer, instead took her mouth with more teeth and anger than finesse. He didn't care. He tangled his hand in her hair, and pulled until her mouth opened beneath him. Still it wasn't enough. Right now, anything short of full-body possession wasn't enough. He dragged his lips where her dress skimmed her breast, sucked hard, marking her. Damn it, she was his. Her hands twisted on the front of his jacket and he heard a whimper come from within her. Fear?

That stopped him. He lifted his head, and stared, frustration and desire beat like a drum behind his eyes. Her lips were swollen where he'd kissed her, her eyes were more shut than open, and her prim little bra peeked out from beneath her not so prim dress.

Still, there was no hiding the victorious gleam in her eye. Somehow that only made it worse. "You did that on purpose," he said.

With trembling hands, she fixed her dress. "Damn straight, Barrington. You sure you have to go?"

Satin sheets. Satin sheets. Satin sheets.

He didn't answer, just tucked her into a cab and then took off for the strain station. The long walk was just what he needed to cool off.

Soon, Amanda. Very soon.

11

THE WEEKEND PASSED in one caffeine-induced blur for Joe, but by the time Monday morning arrived, he was feeling rather proud of himself. He had booked a suite at the Ritz for Saturday night, had a reservation for two at Chanterelle and had arranged for two dozen roses to be delivered to her office on Friday.

Yes, everything was falling into place.

When the final reservation was confirmed, he called Amanda. The weekend would be a surprise. His gift to her. Hopefully, it'd be one she'd never forget.

It was about time he was living up to his potential. Joe arranged to start flying lessons in October. The money would be a little tight, but his crew leader had been great about letting Joe work extra hours.

After twenty-seven years as Avery Barrington's no-account brother, Joe was ready to do something about it. Amanda would be proud.

It was 10:00 a.m. before he finally had a break. Working out on the line was hard work, which was good. They were too busy getting the planes in and out of the gates for him to think about her. Making love to her. Sliding her oh-so-prim bra right off her shoulders and watching her eyes drift with pleasure. He looked at his hands, wishing they weren't so rough, wishing they weren't so...crude.

He stared out the terminal window, wondering why he hadn't been an engineer, or a Wall Street mogul, or some other mogul.

Because he liked planes.

Damn it.

He liked Amanda just as much as planes. Considering the thirty minutes of sleep he'd finally gotten last evening, he suspected he liked Amanda more.

A DC-10 pulled up, ready for take-off. Slowly she cruised down the runway, picking up speed, finally lifting in the air, graceful as a bird. Planes were steady, reliable.

Just like Amanda.

And Joe could be steady and reliable, too.

Planes didn't have feelings.

Unlike Amanda.

He picked up the phone. Steady and reliable—that's who he was.

"Amanda Sedgewick's office."

"Amanda, please."

"May I say who's calling, please?"

"Joe Barrington."

"Oh." The secretary drew the word out five syllables long. Disapproval in four out of the five. Then one, long, heavy sigh, just in case he missed it. "You'd think her boyfriend would know when she's ill, considering this is the first sick day she's taken in six years."

"Sick?" She'd looked healthy on Friday. Sexy, vibrant, alive. In fact, he was getting a little hot just thinking about her physical well-being.

"Yeah, Mr. Joe Not the Doctor, she called this morning, coughing and sneezing, poor doll. Said she spent the night puking her guts out. You would think someone who professes to care for her would be sitting by her bedside, tucking in the covers. You would think someone who enjoys her witty repartee would be bolding her head as she worships the porcelain goddess. You would think that the man she adores would be at her side with chicken noodle soup, and not that pond scum that comes out of a can, neither. Obviously some of the members of the stronger sex do not think at all. I bet Dr. Barrington would not be so crass, Mr. Barrington. Goodbye."

Joe could only stare at the phone.

"Problem, Barrington?"

He didn't know she was sick. Hell. He was innocent here. "Hmm?" He looked up, and there stood his crew leader, Buzz.

"Barrington? Everything all right? You look a little pale." Not everybody could carry off the nickname, Buzz, but Edward Taylor could. He was tough, could stand up to even the most impatient pilots, and when the planes went out, everything was exactly right.

"I'm fine," Joe murmured.

Buzz gestured to the phone in Joe's hand. "Uh, if you're done there, then..."

Joe handed off the receiver. "Can you cover for me? I need to leave. It's an emergency."

Buzz scratched his head, looking doubtful. "Well, we got ten 'PS' checks, one 'B' check on a 737, and there's a 747 that needs a new carbon seal on the gearbox."

"I'll pull double shift tomorrow for anybody that can help. Amanda's sick."

"Who's Amanda?"

"She's my, my..." Joe gave up, not wanting to figure out that answer right now. "I need to be there," was what he ended up with, sure of that one.

"Did you sign off on that little Guppy over at Gate C17?"

Joe nodded.

"All right. But be back in four hours. I've got a 727 coming in that's got a slow oil leak. We're going to try and get it back in the air this afternoon." The crew leader grinned. "I still remember what it was to be in love. Calling home right now."

In love? Yeah, sure. And where in hell would be find homemade chicken noodle soup? "Thanks, Buzz. I'll be back. You're the best."

Joe grabbed his keys and ran out of the ready room, the door slamming behind him.

AMANDA HAD NEARLY finished her first wall when she heard the buzzer. She put down the paint brush and surveyed her handiwork with a critical eye. Not bad for a novice.

Today she was the new Amanda. No more long nights pacing the floors because Joe Barrington didn't feel the need to call her and say "Hello."

"You can't change 'em, honey." Wasn't that what Grace told her? No, she couldn't change Joe, but she could change Amanda.

She waded through the drop cloth and pressed the button. She certainly wasn't expecting company. Might be somebody from work, though. A messenger with the transcripts from the Northcott mediation. She coughed into the intercom. "Yes?"

"Amanda. You okay?"

Joe. She looked at her painting clothes and wanted to cry. Sweatpants and a tank top. Not the best look. "What are you doing here?"

"Let me up and then go lie down. It'll be all right."

Go lie down? What was that all about? Maybe he'd changed his mind. Maybe he was here to ravish her. Obediently, she pressed the button and took one last look at her self.

She opened the door, and there he stood, panting. What was the emergency? Her heart started to lift. Maybe he needed to see her. Maybe that was the emergency.

"Joe? Is everything all right?"

He looked at her, the sweats, the tank top, the can of paint thinner at her feet. "You're painting?"

Well, he wasn't dressed much better. Jeans and

grease-covered shirt. And a wonderful-smelling paper sack. He'd come straight from the airport. With food. "Are you all right?"

He strode into the room, rubbing his face. "I thought you were sick."

And it all made sense. The worry, the out of breathness, the—oh my God, soup. *He'd brought her soup.* She struggled to find the chair under the drop cloths, couldn't find it and settled for leaning against a blob in the middle of the room. It felt like a chair.

He looked around. "What are you doing?"

"I'm painting the apartment." She held out a paint brush. "You can help. Unless you're going to leave now. After you've come all this way to give me...soup," she tried to stay cool, like she didn't care that he had run out on their date and hadn't called her *once* over the weekend, she really did, but the warm smell of chicken noodle soup was turning her into mush, and her voice softened right at the end.

"I'll help." He handed her the brown paper bag. "But only if you eat this first."

How did he do it? She spent the weekend watching the Home Improvement Channel and called her mother four times. Just to chat. Something she'd never done before. Anything to keep her mind off the phone. But no matter what she did, her thoughts always returned to Joe.

Everything between them was so new, so uncertain. She'd planned on seducing Joe, but he'd turned the tables on her—made her fall in love—and he probably didn't even know.

When he gazed at her, a thousand apologies in his eyes, she turned even gooier.

"Deal."

He looked down and stared at her feet. Bare feet with red paint spots. Embarrassed, she curled her toes. It didn't help. Finally, he raised his eyes to her face and waved half-heartedly at the walls. "It looks good."

The walls were as red as red could be, and her vision tended to blur when she stared at them too long, but she'd done it. All by herself. Her apartment was thirty-five percent completely covered in red. Not white, not beige, not taupe, not wheat. Red.

She started to fold her arms across her chest, then remembered she was holding her soup. Hot soup. She placed it on the kitchen table. "Yeah, I think so." Actually, she was beginning to rethink the color scheme, but wasn't quite ready to admit that.

She returned to the living room and he looked down at her feet again. "You sure you need help?"

She shrugged defensively. "No, but you're welcome to stay if you want." She flicked back a strand of hair from her face. "If you have the time."

"Yeah."

"Well." Amanda exhaled and his gaze rested on her chest. The room heated for a moment. "Would you like to eat first or just start painting?"

"Why don't you eat," he answered, still staring at her chest.

Here they were. Alone in her apartment. He'd said "soon"... Suddenly now wasn't even soon enough. She breathed again. Deeper this time. His jaw tightened. "Okay."

He followed her into the small kitchen, off-white with a Danish modern breakfast table. "Do you think I should paint in here, too?"

Joe looked startled, and then cleared his throat. "Nah."

She put two bowls on the table, but he pushed one aside and sat down. "Not hungry. Thanks."

He still looked a little pale. "Smells good."

"You're playing hooky today?"

She nodded. "Yup. It's the new me."

"The old you wasn't all that bad."

She stopped. Checked to see if he was joking, but he looked sincere. "Really?"

"Really."

"Well, that may be, but the times they are a-changing."

"Looks like they're changing to red." He tried to smother his grin, but his lip twitched suspiciously.

Today it didn't bother her at all. "You're laughing at me."

Magically his face transformed. All trace of humor gone, but there was a telltale dimple in his left cheek that hadn't been there before. "No, no."

She felt like laughing herself. "Actually, it's Flambeau Red." She sat down at the table and began to eat. "I may change it."

JOE PICKED UP his paintbrush and surveyed the wall in front of him. Not bad. He'd done lots of painting in his high school days. Now, Amanda, well, obviously she didn't put herself through law school by painting. But for a first effort it wasn't awful.

But red? Paint was everywhere. In her hair, on her feet and on that sinful, white tank top. No, Joe, don't want to think about that. He felt the familiar blood-draining reaction to even a hint of Amanda's flesh and swore.

"Everything okay?" He watched as she climbed down from the ladder she was on, completely unaware of the lurid thoughts running through his head.

"Not a problem," he answered, trying not to look at her chest. She was wearing one of those slinky bras, the kind he didn't understand why women bothered with at all. She was either cold, or charged up, or…he closed his eyes. Damn, he needed to change the subject here.

Satin sheets. That was his new mantra. He had a beautiful scene for seduction all planned out and it didn't include a drop cloth amid paint rollers and turpentine.

Thankfully the phone rang. Amanda picked up the receiver.

"Hello."

She listened for a minute and then turned to him, mouthing, "It's Avery."

Trouble.

"Yes, I'm fine."

He watched her talk, watched her face change from calm to amused. "No, Joe didn't dump me.

"No, I didn't dump him, either. Tell me about Penelope.

"Self-absorbed? No, not really.

"Well, yes, she likes to talk about her job, but I mean, we *all* do that Avery."

She smiled. It was a nice smile. "Yes, even you.

"In the right environment, a man who listens can be quite appealing.

"Yes, Joe's a good listener.

"Maybe you should. Listen, I need to go Avery."

She didn't need to hang up on his account. He was content just to watch her. He sat down against the one remaining white wall and it felt good. He closed his eyes, letting Amanda's voice wash over him.

"No, you don't need to come over. It's just a little runny nose." She sniffed into the phone.

"Yes, he's here.

"No, you're not being a pest. I think you're being sweet. I wish you'd talk to Penelope, though. Maybe send her orchids…"

Orchids, he thought sleepily. Maybe he should send her orchids instead….

WHEN AMANDA hung up the phone, she looked over at Joe. Asleep. He'd looked so tired. What the heck was he doing? And why? Not that it mattered right now, she certainly wasn't going to wake him up. She grabbed a pillow and then put it behind his head. For a few minutes she sat next to him, just watching him sleep.

He didn't stir at all. Well, she could wait. Amanda noticed the red paint that stained her shirt and her feet. Yuck. No wonder he opted for painting instead of making love. That was something she could fix, so she gave him a quick kiss on the cheek and then went off and picked out her sexiest lingerie. Next up, a long shower. Let him sleep a little bit more.

By the time she emerged from the bedroom, Amanda was feeling pretty good. She'd gotten most of the paint off herself, and even painted her toenails.

Hopefully he was awake by now. She closed her eyes and leaned against the doorframe, striking a seductive pose, all ready for him to awake and take her in his arms.

When she was greeted with nothing but silence, she shook her hair and sighed. Loudly. Nothing. Heck, she couldn't even hear him breathe.

Finally, she opened her eyes to survey the situation. The room was exactly the way she'd left it. Open paint cans, rollers and her toolbox. Everything was there.

But Joe.

12

HE CALLED HER on Tuesday afternoon and apologized. He had to work. Again. Amanda tried to sound nice and understanding, but inside she was seething.

"I'll see you Saturday," he said.

"Are you off all day Saturday?" she replied, still trying for that understanding tone. She didn't want to *sound* like she was being sarcastic.

"Not just Saturday, the whole weekend."

"Good. Why don't you pick me up about ten in the morning? I've got an idea."

He laughed in the phone. Just the way it sounded, warm and intimate, gave her goose bumps in places she'd never had before.

After he hung up, she smiled, determined. This time, there would be no question. Joe Barrington, you're going to be seduced.

Amanda called Grace into her office. She needed something one hundred percent guaranteed. She'd tried subtle, she'd tried sexy. Nothing had worked.

Now it was time for the heavy ammunition.

SATURDAY DAWNED warm, breezy, not a cloud in the sky. Joe took his time getting ready. Hot shower, close shave. He had no idea what Amanda had planned for the day, but everything was set up for tonight. He couldn't wait to see her face.

At last she'd see him for what he could be.

He stared at himself in the fogged-up mirror. *What he could be.* He wiped down the mirror, drawing a big *L* on the reflection of his forehead. He didn't want to stop seeing her. Not ever. Why was he working double-shifts now? Because of Amanda. Why was he learning to cook now? Because of Amanda. Why was he watching *Law & Order?* Well, he really liked the show, but because of Amanda, too. Lawyers weren't so bad after all.

God, a guy's ego would really take a beating with her. But wasn't she worth it?

Yeah.

He had disappointed a lot of people in the past, but not anymore.

He rubbed his heart. There was a new weight in there. Hope was a heavy thing. He drew a lightening bolt on the glass and then threw the wet towel on the floor.

Nope, not today. He picked it up, folding it, hanging it up carefully on the rack. If she could change, then so could he.

AMANDA WOULDN'T let him see her until she was dressed, which was bad enough. He was wearing slacks and a button-down shirt. He looked presentable.

And then she came out of the bedroom.

Joe tried to speak, but his tongue was hanging out far enough to lick the floor.

Black skirt.

Little, black skirt.

Heels.

Man-killer, do-me heels.

Her hair rolled down her shoulders in waves, and she was wearing red lipstick. It matched her walls.

A limo was picking them up at six-thirty. Dinner at seven, the hotel at eight. He was supposed to hold out for eight hours and twenty-seven minutes?

He was a dead man.

"Ready to go?" she asked, all casual and cool.

"I think I need to sit down for a minute." And breathe. God, he couldn't breathe. He collapsed into a chair.

She pursed her lips and put on more lipstick. "You get some rest, honey. You're going to need it."

He was a dead man.

WELL, IT WASN'T tea at the Ritz. Instead she took him to Coney Island. Joe hadn't been there since he was a kid. But she knew right where she was going. They bypassed the carousel, the games, the concession stands and the bumper cars. Amanda acted just like a woman on a mission and apparently that mission was the Cyclone.

Joe stared up the old roller coaster and smiled. "You want to go on this?"

"You betcha. Chicken?" she asked, hands on hips.

Somehow he didn't think they were talking about the Cyclone. His blood heated just a bit. Today, they were on his turf. No talk about careers, absolutely nothing but blue skies and black leather. "Never."

They made it through the line and he watched her climb into the car. The leather hugged curves he didn't want to remember she had. He settled in next to her, still trying to figure out what she was doing.

The attendant pulled down the bar and she shook out her hair.

There was not one trace of Amanda Sedgewick in her. Somehow she changed into avenging Valkyrie.

Amanda turned to him, not demure, not shy. Confident, bold and more than a little scary.

"Joe, it's time you learned something about me. You see, under this skirt, I'm wearing Victoria's Secret Second Skin Satin Hipster in Whisper Pink."

Joe gripped the bar a little tighter. "Okay."

"I've got seven pairs just like this at home."

He cut her off. "I don't think talking about your underwear is a good idea."

The car started to move away from the platform. "No, actually, it's an excellent idea. You think of me as Whisper Pink. I'm fragile. The little princess." She licked her lips.

He looked up at the sky, down at the ocean below

them, anywhere but at that succulent mouth. "I don't think that."

"You don't need to lie about it. It's okay. You're right." She reached her hands under her skirt and shimmied in her seat.

Joe simply sat, frozen.

The roller coaster started to climb up the long, long hill, creaking all the way, the chain grating against the steel track. And Amanda slid a pair of Whisper Pink Second Skin Hipsters down her long, long legs.

He whimpered.

"But you see," she went on, ignoring his heart attack in the making, "I can change. You can change. What we think we are," she held up the panties like a battle flag, "isn't always what we have to be."

Two boys behind them clapped Joe on the back. "Dude!"

The car stopped, poised in midair.

Amanda stared him down.

Joe couldn't move, couldn't think, couldn't breathe.

One pair of Whisper Pink Hipsters billowed in the breeze.

And then the car dropped down the hill, gravity taking over, and the one pair of Hipsters swirled away.

Oh, God. He was trapped on a roller coaster with Amanda in black leather, no panties and a "take-no-prisoners" gleam in her eyes. He felt so sorry for any defense attorney she ever went up against. They were going to lose.

They swirled around loops and up camel-back hills, round a curve, and Joe's stomach was left somewhere back at that first hill.

Amanda threw her arms in the air and screamed. Joe just gripped the bar in front of him, needing distance, needing to run. But on the Cyclone, a man could go nowhere but down.

Finally, mercifully, they made it back to the station. Joe scrambled out and watched warily as Amanda extended one leg, placing it carefully on the wooden planking. Next came another. *Something else.* All he needed to do was think of something else.

Anything. He looked up at the skies and a pair of Whisper Pink panties floated in the breeze, drifting out toward the Atlantic Ocean.

He was a dead man.

AMANDA HAD DONE IT. She walked along the boardwalk with a confidence, a flair, a freedom that she'd never felt before. Every inch of her felt alive, the salty sea air teasing her nose. Everywhere she looked there was color, bright Technicolor. Neon-red. Lemon-yellow. Not an ivory, buff, or wheat to be found anywhere.

She ate cotton candy, had their picture taken, bought an I Love N.Y. T-shirt, and all in all was having a grand time.

Joe looked marvelous in the picture. He couldn't

take his eyes off her, and there, in an 8×11, was positive proof that she could stare at anytime she felt like it. She bought two.

"I think I should take up photography, don't you?" she asked. She liked the idea of capturing them together on paper.

"Hmm?" he said, dragging his eyes from her legs.

She touched his chest with a scarlet-covered nail. "I think I'm going to take up photography."

"Photography? That's nice."

Only one more thing could make this day absolutely perfect.

"Joe?" She stopped walking, admiring the balloons and ribbons that adorned a carnival game. A father started shooting the targets for his little girl. "Have I proven my point yet?"

He stood a careful twenty-four inches away from her. Not far, but not close enough. "What point is that?"

"There's absolutely no reason in this world why we shouldn't make love."

The dazed look faded and he looked at his watch. Six and a half more hours. "No."

She flipped a dollar down on the counter and the pot-bellied little attendant scooped it up. "I'm thinking it's time."

The man winked at her and pressed the button on the water gun in front of her.

Amanda bent over and lined up her sight with the

clown targets, her thighs tingling from the warm air. The buzzer sounded and she began to shoot.

"What the hell are you doing?"

"I'm trying to win a prize."

Joe moved to stand behind her, blocking the view. She wiggled for effect. Obligingly, he moved closer. "Dammit, Amanda."

Her aim misfired and the water shot into the air. "You could help me."

He wrapped himself around her, muttering something she couldn't understand. The bulge that was pressing behind her, she understood quite well. If her smile was a little fundamental, who could blame her? Finally, the buzzer stopped, the little man rang the bell. "We have a winner!"

Amanda picked a fuzzy-headed little troll and shot Joe a grin. "What do we do next?"

"A cold dip in the ocean would fix me."

Victory was near. "How about the Wonder Wheel instead?"

JOE THOUGHT the cars on the Ferris wheel were four sizes too small. She sat next to him, her legs stretched out, crossing her legs first one way then the other. He tried to keep his thoughts pure, but the little voice inside was head was starting to whisper lewd suggestions.

Determined to ignore them, he stuck his head out of the car and watched the streets of Brighton Beach.

This was *not* what he had planned.

A hand drifted to his thigh.

The world started to spin and he closed his eyes.

"Joe?"

"What?"

"Don't you like me?"

He pretended ignorance. "I think you're nice."

She slid closer, the sound of leather rubbing against the warm metal. "I don't want to be nice. I don't want to fragile, I don't want to be a princess, or even Mary Sunshine."

Mary Sunshine? "What?"

Her hand rubbed his thigh. He swallowed. Hard.

"I want to be desirable, and sexy and, well, just a little bit bad."

"Bad?" His voice cracked.

"Joe, I need you." The hand rubbing continued. Her lips feathered against his ear. "Make love to me, Joe."

AMANDA HELD her breath. Joe didn't move. The car continued to rock back and forth, and she wondered if she'd blown it.

"Joe?"

He turned to look at her and she saw such pure pain, she wanted to cry. He didn't love her, he didn't want to make love to her. All she'd done was embarrass herself.

And then he moved. His body closed in tight.

"Amanda, I've got to ask you something first."

"Anything," she whispered, mesmerized by the

feverish frustration in his eyes. She covered his heart with her hand. Under her palm, the heavy beat thrilled her.

"Why me? Out of all the guys, why am I the one?"

She bit her lip, not knowing whether she should tell him the truth or even if he'd believe her. What was it about Joe that made her sacrifice her pride? Why Joe? Eggs Benedict, *Harry Potter* and the freedom to finally discover who she was. The answer was really simple.

"I love you."

JOE HAD PREPARED himself for a lot of answers, but that wasn't one of them. He couldn't take it if this was a joke. He'd thought she'd been playing with him, wanting nothing more than a walk on the wild side. Now all the sudden, the stakes had changed.

"Amanda." Forty thousand reasons sprang to his lips why they shouldn't be together, but he didn't have the heart to say one.

He thought he had everything set up perfectly. A romantic evening, wine, candlelight. Now he was going to screw that up, too.

He took her face in his hands and kissed her. At first, he was hesitant. This was Amanda. Even with a tight skirt, and hooker lips, she was more precious than anyone he'd ever known. He brushed his lips across hers. Once, twice. He tugged gently at her bottom lip, trying not to rush her, trying to hold back. She sighed and her mouth opened beneath him.

Sweetly. He stroked her face, her hair. She smelled so good, so warm. Even the smell of leather couldn't mask her basic scent.

He dove into the kiss, taking his time; they were going nowhere, just riding into the air, a meeting of lips. He felt the tip of her tongue touch his own and he smiled against her mouth. "Not yet. We have all afternoon, and right now, I don't want to do anything but taste you."

She groaned and pressed in closer. Up in the air, the world seemed so far away. They were alone in a magical place, and no one could touch them here.

His finger trailed down her neck, down her throat. He felt a shiver. Her skin was so soft, so white. Like marble. He touched her pulse beating in her throat. Yet so alive. Her blood was pumping fast and heavy. For him.

"I'm taking you home when we get down, Amanda. I want to see you, taste you. I've been dreaming about you, Amanda. I tried to stay away from you, but I can't. I'm done fighting this." He pushed aside her shirt, smiling at the whisper-thin bra that covered her breasts. "You slayed me the first time I saw you without the robe." He took her nipples in his hands, watching her cheeks flush as he rolled them between his fingers.

"What do you want?" he asked her, bending his head to kiss her once more.

In answer, she climbed in his lap, her legs straddling him, and she started to unbutton his shirt. His body struggled for control, aching to push inside her, right there. When she looked up at him, her eyes were fever-bright. "I want you to touch me. You have to touch me."

He nearly came. "We're almost to the ground."

"I don't care."

Truth be told, he didn't care either, but then the car rolled to a stop.

Quickly, he buttoned up her shirt, his hands fumbling, doing a poor job of it. "We'll go home."

She nodded. "Yes."

THE SUBWAY CAR was packed, and they had to stand. Everyone was heading into the city for a bright Saturday afternoon. Amanda held tight against the pole, the train swaying back and forth. She watched Joe from underneath her lashes, wondering what he was thinking. He met her gaze, his eyes flaring with arousal.

That was a look she understood.

She stood frozen, trapped by the heat in his eyes. His heavy stare wandered over her, touching her lips, her breasts, her thighs.

Slowly, he leaned closer, his arm brushing against her chest. The slight touch was a heady torment, and her breasts swelled, her nipples throbbing against her bra.

Everything inside her felt heavy and full, all rushing down to the apex of her thighs. It was another fifteen minutes to her apartment, and she didn't think she could wait. She slid against the pole, oh so carefully, but it only made it worse. She heard Joe's indrawn breath.

A couple of teenagers made their way to the door, pushing Amanda closer to Joe.

He cradled her body with his own, grazing his lips over her neck. She rubbed against him, and gentleman that he was, he locked his hands on her hips and pushed against her. His erection was hard and insistent, and she licked her lips, her eyes drifting shut.

Her legs started to shake, threatening collapse, but he held her tight. There was something incredible about the way he smelled. All musky and male. Each time she moved, he answered. Each time he moved, she moaned.

His hand skimmed lower, flirting between them. A woman with a Bloomingdale's bag stared at them, before looking away.

Amanda really didn't care. All she wanted was release from the insistent throbbing between her legs. She rocked again his hand, biting her lip in frustration.

His hand slid between her legs higher and higher, and without hesitation she parted them. Anything.

Her stomach pumped, waiting.

One heartbeat, then two.

One finger slid inside her, then two. His fingers pushed inside her farther, and she leaned against him fully, her legs useless. She shivered, cold, then hot.

His lips brushed against her ear. "You are so wet."

Oh.

Slowly he pulled his fingers inside and out of her, and her muscles contracted around him, trying to hold him, not wanting him to stop. She closed her eyes, taking deep breaths, feeling the dampness inside her. When she opened her eyes, she tried to focus, but she saw nothing.

She was surrounded by people, but it didn't register.

He toyed with the outside of her lips, teasing, tickling. "No," she whispered.

"You don't like that, hmm?"

Once more, he put his fingers inside her, pushing upwards. He went deeper this time as his long fingers circled, sensing the coils of tension racking her body. She tried to keep her hips still, keep them from following the rhythm of his hand, riding to meet him. But she couldn't.

He kissed her neck, whispering in her ear, in slow, exquisite detail exactly what he was going to do to her. What he wanted to do with her right here. Right under the watchful eyes of everyone around them.

Oh.

She chewed on her lip, ready to scream. When his thumb brushed against her, she felt her muscles shake and spasm. He covered her mouth with his own. That was all she could take. She closed her eyes, and watched the world shatter.

And he kissed away her cries.

13

THEY MADE IT to her lobby, made it to her elevator. He took her keys and undid the locks, and then Hallelujah, they were inside.

He pulled up her skirt, her hands fumbling with his fly.

"Condom," he said, just as she was pulling down his zipper.

"Bathroom."

"Don't move."

She stayed there, plastered against the door, waiting. "Hurry."

"Where is it?"

She started to count. "Top drawer, left-hand side."

One. Two. He was back. "I can't wait," he said, taking her lips in a quick kiss.

She fumbled with his briefs. "Now."

He sheathed himself with shaking fingers. "I wanted this to be slow," he said, lifting her.

She wrapped her legs around his waist, needing to feel him inside her. "Later."

He took one step forward, braced her against the door, she locked her hands around his nape.

And then he plunged inside her.

JOE STAGGERED for a second, amazed by the sheer overwhelming pleasure of being surrounded by Amanda. Warm, drenching pleasure. There was no ice or coldness in her, only a heat that made him frantic. He needed to find control, but all his control was gone.

Now she was his. *Finally*. Her hips ground against him, and he started to move. Thrusting inside her, deeper, as if he could touch her heart.

His eyes held her crystal-blue gaze, unflinching. The way she looked at him, with need and something more, made anything possible. For now, nothing could touch them.

She was his.

He drove inside her, over and over, determined to please her. In this, there would be no one but him.

Joe kissed her again, her tongue tangling with his, her breathing as ragged as his own.

Over and over.

Her head rolled to one side, her hair falling across his arm, just like his dreams. She bit her lip, and still he moved.

Over and over. Not yet.

A moan of surrender broke her lips. She was close. Her nails were biting into his neck, but there was no pain. Instead, he moved faster, harder.

He felt her muscles clench around her, saw her eyes go blank, her lashes drift downward. She began to gasp and shiver, and he smiled with satisfaction.

At last.

He thrust inside her one last time, as far as he could go. His body jerked, a charge of energy pulsing through him. Then his climax came, the undeniable pleasure, the undeniable truth.

He loved her.

THE SUN DIPPED low in the sky, the rays reaching through the blinds making long, even stripes on the satin sheets.

Satin sheets. Even his dreams weren't close enough.

Amanda rose above him, her hair turning gold, her body pure silver.

"You look so perfect, like something Michelangelo created and then hid from the world. I would have done that, too."

She didn't answer, only smiled, her lips curving in a woman's smile of pleasure. She splayed her hands on his chest, her fingers kneading him like a cat's. Slowly her hips moved up and then down, embracing him with liquid fire. Her mouth trailed over him, silken flesh over hard, unforgiving muscle.

This wasn't right. It was her turn now. He rolled her beneath him, taking her mouth in a gentle kiss. He thrust into her with quiet passion, gently as he had longed to do, as she deserved.

He kissed her neck, then her breasts, watching her chest rise as her breathing grew labored.

She murmured his name, a single sound separated

from the rest of the city noise. The air conditioner hummed, a plane flew overhead, but he heard little except the beat of her heart. Her head twisted, as if she was fighting, and Joe covered her mouth once more, thrust harder, deeper. He reached between them, found the place that brought her release.

When she moaned, he found his release, and then pulled her close, watching her as her breathing slowed, as her eyes drifted shut in sleep. And even then he held tight. He wasn't about to let her go. Not now.

THE BUZZER RANG exactly at six-thirty. Amanda didn't wake. Quietly, Joe slipped from the sheets, and went to the intercom and told the driver to go home. It wasn't exactly what he planned, somehow his plans had always gotten off-track. He'd make it up to her. She deserved romance and candlelight.

He checked his watch. There was a drugstore down the street. Maybe he could give her romance and candlelight after all.

AMANDA ROLLED OVER in her bed, reaching out for Joe. Empty. Then she heard the music. Nina Simone. A smile lifted the corners of her mouth. What was that about? She wrapped herself in the sheet and wandered to the living room.

But she hadn't wandered into her living room—she'd made her way to wonderland. Candles were everywhere, flickering, bathing the room in a magical glow.

He was sitting on her couch, sipping a glass of wine, casually, as if he'd done nothing at all.

The room dimmed with the blur of her tears.

At the rustling sound of the sheet, he turned and lifted a brow. As one song came to a close, he stood, walked over, and then took her hand. "Dance?"

She didn't answer, just floated into his arms. They whirled around the room, with no sounds but the hiss of the candles and the soft slide of satin over marble.

One song wafted into another, and before long the music stopped.

She studied his face, so unbearably dear, so unbelievably handsome and let the sheet fall to the floor.

At first he didn't move, and instead let his gaze linger long and slow, making her blush. He lifted his hand and trailed a gentle finger from her mouth, down the line of her throat, between her breasts and lower.

"I owe you an apology," he said quietly.

"For what?"

He took the sheet and draped it over the couch, then lifted her in his arms. "I should have done this at the start. Sometimes I'm a little slow."

"I like it when you're a little slow."

Gently, he lay her down, the satin cool as it slid against her skin. "Good," he murmured, his mouth cruising over her throat, and then her breasts, heavy with intent. Her fingers lifted to the buttons on his shirt, but he grabbed her wrist and shook his head. "This is for you."

Helpless to do much more, Amanda closed her eyes. His rough palms grazed her breasts and she lifted up to meet his touch. For long torturous moments, he did nothing but lightly circle her nipples with wicked strokes of his fingers. She felt the moisture pool inside her, pulsing and throbbing.

He lowered his head, his mouth replacing his fingers, and she shoved her fingers in his hair, pressing him close. His tongue flicked against her skin, at first gentle, sensual, and then with more purpose. His mouth pulled her nipples in deeper, almost painful, and she cried out.

Amanda curled her toes, her thighs falling open, waiting for him to appease her. But he chose to ignore her pleadings and instead his mouth worked its way farther down, his tongue teasing against her belly.

Oh, please.

His fingers stroked the inside of her thigh. High, but not high enough. He cupped her heat and she curled her hips into his hand waiting to be filled.

But he had other plans. He slid his hands beneath her legs, opening her even wider. His mouth pleasured the inside of her thighs, licking the moisture that coated them. With each flick of the tongue he moved closer, and she fisted her hands in the sheet.

Sounds, more like incoherent pleas, broke from

her lips as she felt herself flying higher and higher. She bucked against him, her muscles clenching and unclenching.

Just a little bit more.

While his mouth continued its torment, he put his fingers inside her, touching her *there*.

And that was enough.

The lights behind her eyes gleamed red and gold and she felt her muscles shake. She cried out just as her senses exploded.

THEY DIDN'T LEAVE her apartment that weekend and on Sunday afternoon they'd just finished lunch when she got the phone call. It was a retired secretary from Clean-All returning Amanda's call. When Amanda hung up the phone, she was flushed with her success.

"Good news?" he asked, like he couldn't tell.

She sat down on the couch next to him, her hands automatically straightening the Sunday paper. "The best. She knows where the old files are. I knew we'd get him, and now there's undisputable proof. We *have* to celebrate."

He bet she celebrated a lot. She worked so hard for her success. "And what would you like to do?"

She pulled her hair back with one hand, her breasts lifting, reminding him that she wore no bra. "Dinner tonight at Chanterelle, champagne."

And orchids. Tonight he'd give her the orchids.

"I'll make reservations." He started to rise from the couch, but she pushed him back.

"Not yet." Her cool blue eyes were awash with purpose. He was getting to recognize that look. Joe might never have been the brightest in school, but he knew how to pleasure a woman.

Amanda pulled her T-shirt over her head and climbed into his lap. His hands found the places she wanted to be touched, his mouth kissed her in the exact right way. It wasn't everything he wanted to give her, but right now it was all he had.

MONDAY MORNING came way too soon. Joe had set the alarm for 3:00 a.m. He had to make it home, shower and get in to work. Amanda was still fast asleep. He watched her sleep, the city lights keeping the room from darkness, even at this hour.

She loved him. He hadn't brought it up again, he was too afraid she would change her mind. He gathered up his clothes and started to dress. He still didn't understand it all. The one big question lurked out there. What now? She was going to win Vincent's case for him, go out and conquer the world. And what was wrong with him? Why couldn't he be proud? Why couldn't he get past the fact that second place was really okay?

After all, he'd done second place his entire life.

He pulled on his boots with more force than necessary and started to walk out the door.

Amanda rolled in the white satin sheets and his heart twisted.

God, he loved her.

He leaned down over the bed, stroked the hair away from her face. He pressed a gentle kiss against her cheek and then walked out the door.

AMANDA WANDERED into work at 9:45 a.m... *9:45 a.m.* One hour and forty-five minutes after Powers. It was going to be on the news, she just knew it. Nobody said anything, though, and she was somewhat disappointed that no one had noticed.

She'd searched her apartment for a note from Joe, but couldn't find anything. Oh, well. He'd call. By eleven o'clock, she'd heard nothing. It was still early. By 4:45, she was ready to cry. Thankfully, Grace was nearby, adorned with an Empire State Building monument hanging around her neck.

"Grace, do you know a place to get a drink around here?"

Grace looked up from her desk. "Well, Caruso's is just around the corner, and there's always O'Malleys. You looking for someplace sophisticated or a little boisterous?"

"Boisterous." She couldn't handle sophisticated today.

"O'Malley's is the place. They have the *best* bartender. His name is Joaquin, and he's trying to be an actor. Oh, my God. He is to die for." Grace fanned herself. "Oh, but I bet you're taking your new beau. Chef Joe. Probably wouldn't be the best choice."

"No, I'm going alone. Unless you'd like to come?" she asked hopefully.

Grace saw through her. "Oh, boss. He's done it, hasn't he? He broke your heart. Look at you, poor dear."

"He didn't call today." She felt pitiful and needy, but after the weekend they'd had, surely...

"Oh, it's the worst." Grace clicked her tongue.

"I thought he'd at least leave a note."

"They just get so wrapped up in themselves, they forget that we need a little reassurance."

"I told him I loved him."

Grace adjusted her hair. "Oh, honey. You've been betrayed, but you can't let this get you down, you know what I mean? It's the time of year. You got baseball, college ball starting up, and even preseason for the pros. And what woman can compete with sports? Some legends say Mae West had an off-season right after Labor Day. It's a fundamental truth."

This insecurity was new to Amanda, and she felt tears in her eyes. "I don't even know if he likes sports."

Grace took her by the arm. "Come on, honey. You're just a babe to the wolves. Let Aunt Gracey tell you how it is."

O'MALLEY'S WAS PACKED. The air was heavy with smoke and the hum of laughter and conversation.

Every thirty minutes, Amanda excused herself to go the ladies' room. She didn't think Grace was buying it, but she checked her answering machine faithfully.

"You have no messages."

What had she done?

She worked her way through the crowds back to their table. "I want to call him."

Grace slapped her hand over Amanda's. "No. Give me your cell phone."

Amanda hesitated.

"Now. It's for your own good."

Grace picked up the cell phone, just as it started to ring.

Amanda's heart lifted. "It's him."

Grace looked at the caller ID. "Dr. Barrington." She pushed the green button. "Dr. Barrington, I presume? Yes, Amanda is right here. Would you like to speak with her? No, I'm her personal assistant, legal assistant, advice counselor and drinking confidant."

She covered the mouthpiece. "It's for you honey. The doctor."

Amanda took the phone. "Avery?"

"Amanda, have you seen Joe? I was supposed to meet him for an evening out on the town, but he seems to have been detained."

She had hoped he knew. Hoped he had some message for her. Pitiful. "No, I don't know where he is."

"Are you all right? Your voice sounds rather faint."

"It's the noise in the bar, Avery. I'll try and speak up."

"Quite all right. If you see Joe, tell him that I'm waiting."

The phone clicked, and Amanda pushed the little red button. She was a lawyer; she tried to create logical reasons for his behavior. She did it all the time. "He was supposed to meet Avery tonight. Maybe that's why he didn't say anything. Maybe he knew he had plans and he couldn't see me."

"Oh, boss. A girl has got to see the truth as it exists. It's classic."

"I think I'm going to cry."

"Go ahead, boss. I'll get you a Ricky Martini. It'll make you feel better."

FOR THE FIRST TIME in his twenty-seven years, Joe was looking forward to spending time with his brother. But, they had three extra planes come in, and he was running late.

Finally he hooked up with him, Avery looking completely out of place wearing a suit and tie at Blue Velvet. Joe slid into a chair, beer in hand. "Hey, bro."

"Hello. You're late."

"Got tied up at work. Sorry. You're more surly than usual."

"I'm sorry, I had a burn patient today. A little boy, but he's going to be fine."

Oh. Joe clenched his hands, then slid his beer

across the table. "Here. You need this more than I do. I really am sorry."

"I talked to Amanda."

Joe looked at Avery. What did that mean? "Oh? She called?"

"No, I called. I was looking for you."

"I was working," he answered casually, eager to know how she was.

"I expected to find you together."

"No. She's got a life. A busy one."

"What's wrong with you, Joe?"

"Hey, what could be wrong?"

"You're being more of an idiot than usual. You have a wonderful girl with an illustrious career who obviously cares for you. What could be wrong?"

"Yeah, Amanda's perfect, isn't she?"

Avery watched a girl across the bar. When she smiled at him, he smiled in return. Then he turned back to Joe. "What's the real problem?"

Avery would never understand. "You know, Avery, I thought I'd never meet someone more successful than you, but I think Amanda's even got you whooped." He tried to make a joke out of the whole thing.

Avery quirked a brow, looking completely unfazed. "That's a problem?"

"Hell, yes."

"Why?" Avery assumed the doctor persona.

"I think I should buy a car. Maybe a Japanese import. It's not Mercedes, or BMW, but it'd be good to get around town."

"You don't need a car, Joe."

"What? Everybody can have a car but me?"

Avery sighed. "No. All I'm saying is that you don't have need of a car. Is that why you've been working so much? You can't finance it like the rest of the world, you have to pay cash?"

"No, I've got my flying lessons scheduled to start next month. And I've been thinking of moving. Someplace uptown."

"Flying lessons? Hmm. I thought you liked your apartment. If I had known you weren't happy there, I would have helped you move a long time ago."

"I can't see you schlepping boxes, bro."

"Of course not. That's what movers are for." Avery took a sip of beer. "Why all this now? Is this because of Amanda?"

"Some. I'd always figured that I'd get married some day. Live a simple, quiet life somewhere."

Avery rolled his eyes.

"Well, you know what I'm saying here. Avery, you're a tough act to follow, so I didn't even try, because I can't. If anything, it's worse with Amanda. Now I want to try."

"Your machismo is so exaggerated that you cannot tolerate the idea of a woman being more successful?"

It sounded incredibly pitiful. "Maybe."

"Joe, she loves you for who you are."

And who was that? Joe, the wrench-bender, or Joe the incredible lover, or Joe the wanna-be pilot? Somehow he doubted it was Joe the wrench-bender that was her Prince Charming. "You really think she loves me?"

"You're my brother, aren't you? Why shouldn't she?" After Joe's silence, he leaned forward. "What? No pithy remark? No witty comeback?"

What was that from? Joe thought for a minute. *"Thunderball?"*

"Goldeneye. A classic."

A classic? Joe scoffed. "Sean Connery was the best."

"Of course he was. However, Pierce Brosnan has certainly given him a run for his money," Avery explained.

"Want to shoot some pool?"

"You're buying the beer this time, I hope?"

Already Joe felt better. She loved him. That's what was important. He smiled. "Yeah."

"I'd be delighted."

IT WAS MIDNIGHT and O'Malleys was still crowded. Amanda was on her fifth drink and she was going to be sick. Grace looked fine, all three of her.

"You know, Oprah had a whole season on why guys run. Supposedly it's some survival instinct, when they feel threatened. I myself have a theory."

"Waz that?" Amanda focused on the spinning Graces, but the world started to tilt.

"I need to get you home."

SOMEWHERE IN the middle of the night Amanda became aware of another person in her apartment.

"Amanda? It's Joe."

"You rat. You stinkin' rat. You're nothing more than Draco Valdemort Dursey." Her stomach started to heave. "I need...I'm going to be sick." She lurched toward the bathroom.

The toilet loomed in front of her. "Joe. Help."

A warm towel brushed against her forehead. "It's all right, love."

"No, it's not all right." She emptied her stomach in the bowl, and felt a soft hand on her hair. "Don't leave me."

"I'll be right here. Promise."

THE NEXT MORNING, Amanda's alarm blasted off at four-thirty, just like every day. Only today it hurt. She took a shower, and got dressed, cursing anything that contained alcohol, including her eye makeup remover. When she got to the living room she stopped. There was Joe, asleep on her couch.

So it hadn't been a dream. He had really shown up. Late, no call, no note, but still here. Then she realized all her anger had faded away.

She smiled until her head started pounding again and then steadied herself against a chair. Mercifully she made it to the kitchen and got juice and crackers. It wasn't Eggs Benedict, but then she didn't think she could handle Eggs Benedict today. She sat down next to him, just watching him sleep for a bit.

He looked so content. So peaceful. He'd been that way when she first proposed the big plan. Lately though, he'd been tense and anxious. Just like the millions of other minions who worked too hard.

She wrote him a quick note and then went out the door.

JOE MAINTAINED a routine of sorts. He'd show up every night at Amanda's, nothing too early, nothing too late. They'd make love, and then early in the morning, someone would sneak out first. He increased his hours, took some more midnight shifts.

Lots of things were not talked about. Conversation stayed on innocent subjects—art, the pending settlement in Vincent's case.

At some point in time they were going to have to talk, but for now Joe spent most of his waking hours at work. Which was good, because the less he thought of Amanda's turbo-charged success, the better he felt.

By late September, Joe had become quite good at avoiding serious conversations with Amanda. But that didn't stop Avery. Joe had met up with him at Blue Velvet. Avery was becoming a regular; he seemed to really like it. Joe barely had time to eat nowadays, but tonight was Avery's birthday.

"I haven't seen Amanda recently. Why don't we all go to dinner?"

Joe grabbed a handful of pretzels. He'd worked through lunch and he was starving. "Can't. Gotta work."

Avery looked around the bar, the healthy sign of a guy scoping the place out. "Why?"

"I'm thinking of taking Amanda to the Caribbean. I think it'd be good for her to get away for awhile."

Avery didn't even raise an eyebrow. "How are the lessons going?"

That he loved. For a couple hours a week he could fly in the heavens and feel like he was on top of the world. These days it seemed like that was the only time he ever felt on top of the world. And he knew that was wrong. He knew that wasn't the way it was supposed to be. "Pretty good. I should have my license middle of next year. Found a co-op in the city, too."

"You're doing very well."

"Yeah, it's time I grew up." Joe's hand drummed on the table, as he searched for the waitress. "I've been thinking about going to school. You think I could be a broker?"

"Did Amanda ask you to do this?"

He really needed some coffee. "No, but I'm getting kinda tired of working at the airport. It gets old. I want to do something new."

"You're very determined to make this work, aren't you?"

He was going to make it work, no matter what, no matter what. If he kept repeating it to himself, maybe it would all work out. But most days he worried because he just couldn't keep up with her.

Finally the waitress appeared. Joe ordered a cup of coffee and smiled. "I learned it from you."

On October 15th, at exactly 2:14 p.m., Amanda watched, quite pleased with herself, as Vincent D'Antoni signed the settlement papers. He'd be set for life, Clean-All would quietly contact all the airlines who used their products in the mid-eighties, and the rest of the Vincent D'Antoni's of the world would finally see justice.

By 4:15, the entire law firm of Brown, Powers and McGlynn was happily ensconced in the lobby bar at the Waldorf-Astoria. Powers proposed a toast, with a rousing round of "hear, hear" echoing all around. For Amanda, if was a nice victory—she just wished Joe had been able to make it.

Once the congratulations had quieted down, Powers pulled Amanda aside. This was it.

She adjusted her jacket, and wished she'd worn something a little more professional than the forest-green suit.

"Amanda, you know you've been considered for partner for some time."

Yep, here it comes. Amanda smiled. "Yes, sir. You've made that quite obvious."

"Well, this case has far exceeded our expectations—the publicity we'll receive, the potential for future litigation. The partnership is yours if you'd like it."

Partner. Just what she'd waited so long to hear. She waited for the zing of accomplishment, the surge of power she'd feel from being partner. After feeling nothing, she waited a little longer, sure that a tidal wave of success was going to overwhelm her at any moment.

No tidal wave. No nothing.

"Now of course you'll have an equity stake, and we'd hope that you'd be able to bring in some new business for the firm, but that takes time."

It all sounded very exciting, but Amanda had one thing on her mind. "Edward, may I ask you something?"

"Anything."

"It's about my schedule. I don't know that I can put in any more time." As it was, she didn't spend enough time with Joe. She wasn't willing to give up any more.

"I've been meaning to talk to you about that. I've seen too many lawyers suffering from burnout, and I don't want to see that happen to you. You've been carrying a huge case load, Amanda. I've already talked to the others and we'll be hiring several new legal assistants. One of them is yours. It'll mean fewer hours for you."

Fewer hours. She couldn't believe it. He actually wanted her to work less. But she wasn't willing to gamble with Joe. "You mean that?"

He nodded.

She wanted to throw her arms around his neck, but that wouldn't do at all. Instead, she wrung his hand, until he got embarrassed and cleared his throat and she realized what she was doing. "In that case, you've got a deal."

"Partner," she said to herself, testing the word out on her tongue.

When she turned around, there was Joe.

And now the day was perfect.

IT WAS AFTER dark before they made it home. Joe picked up some orchids on the way. It seemed fitting for the occasion. After all, it wasn't every day that his girl made partner.

In her apartment she walked with a cocky swagger. "Can you believe it?"

"I didn't doubt it for a minute," he said, which was absolutely the truth. Whatever she put her mind to, she did. Whatever she wanted, she worked until she got it. And all that seemed to make her happy.

It was the happy part that he didn't understand.

"I couldn't have done this without you," she said, throwing her arms around his neck.

"You're kidding yourself."

"No, I'm serious. Do you know how much I love you?"

"Why don't you show me?" he asked, slipping easily into Incredible Lover Joe persona.

She made love to him the way she did everything.

Absolutely perfectly. When he was inside her, he forgot that he wasn't happy being anything but an airline mechanic. He forgot that he didn't want to be a broker on Wall Street. He forgot everything but her.

It was a long while later, when she was drifting off to sleep that he brushed a kiss against her hair. He whispered a quiet, "I love you" in her ear, and this time he wrote a short note for her to find.

> I love you, but I can't be with you anymore. I'm sorry, I really did try. For you, I would have done anything. But still I don't think it would ever have been enough.

It wasn't easy, but Joe had been kidding himself. He couldn't compete with her. It was beyond stupid to even try. He twisted and angled to turn himself into something that he wasn't, and tonight as she stood there, glowing with all her success, he realized there was absolutely nothing more he could do.

He didn't want to hurt her, but the man she was in love with wasn't him. She'd figure that out soon enough and then where would they be? Once again, he'd be Joe the disappointment.

Joe was out of options.

He left an orchid on top of the note and took one last look. Moonbeams shone on her satin sheets, as if even the heavens adored her. His heart withered inside his chest. Time to go. And so he left, leaving her and the moonbeams behind.

AMANDA WOKE, and reached out for Joe. Empty. She sniffed, waiting for the aroma of Eggs Benedict to tickle her nose. Nothing. Well, this didn't look good. Frowning, she climbed out of bed and wandered into the living room and the kitchen. Nothing.

She went back into the bedroom and then she saw the note. As she read, her smile faded. She sank back into bed and curled into a ball. Two hours passed before she was able to make it to the phone.

She dialed the one person in the world who had never let her down. "Hi, Mom. It's Amanda. Guess what? Got some good news and some bad news..." That was all she could say before she started to cry.

ON SUNDAY she was ready to confront him. He had said he loved her. They could do anything if they loved each other. Love conquered all. Love is blind. A thousand trite phrases all spun in her head.

When she rang his bell, she had her speech all ready.

Joe opened the door. "Hey."

One simple word of greeting and her prepared speech suddenly didn't feel right. "Hey."

They both went inside and he nodded his head in the direction of the couch. Quietly she sat. It was the first time she'd been back to his apartment since the night they'd watched the movie. That was a lifetime ago.

She tried to smile at him, but he watched her with such a solemn look in his eyes that she couldn't.

"Don't you think you should have talked to me about this?"

Joe slumped in his chair. he looked so tired. "It's my issue. I thought I could fix it. I was wrong."

"And what *is* the issue?"

He was silent for long moments, and finally he spoke. "I should be happy for you. I want to be happy for you. But I can't. I can't keep up and it's tearing me apart."

"You don't have to compete with me, Joe."

Today his eyes didn't gleam at all, instead they were dull with sadness. "I didn't compete with Avery. It took me some time to realize that, but then I found my little piece of life that I was happy with. That I was good at. I had kinda resigned myself to it, but then I met you. I wanted to be more for you."

She sat forward, willing him to understand. "You don't have to do that. Not for me. I love you like you are, Joe."

The pain in his eyes brought tears to her own.

"Do you? What if some other guy comes along? Maybe he's a little more successful than me. Another lawyer. A doctor. Do I get compared to him?"

"There's only one of you, Joe. I can't compare you to anyone."

"But I do." He ground the heel of his hand against his head. "I'm so sorry about this. I didn't want to hurt you. I thought we could keep things simple."

"You were wrong."

"That's nothing new."

"Can't you go back to the way you were?"

"Yeah, sure. For a while. But jealousy is a shrewd demon. It comes back around just when you least expect it."

She'd never had a case she thought she couldn't win. Never a challenge she wasn't up for. And sitting across from her was her biggest challenge, her heart. And she couldn't do a damn thing. "I love you."

His mouth twisted. "I love you, too. I didn't want to tell you. At first I was scared. And then later I realized why lawyers don't marry airline mechanics."

There was one thing she could do. "What if I gave it up? I don't have to be partner."

He stood and then paced around the room. "Amanda, don't do that."

"You mean more to me than being partner."

Joe started to laugh. "God, this is rich. You're going to turn down every lousy good thing in your life, just so I can feel better about myself."

"I don't want to live without you."

"I don't want to live without you, either. But Amanda I want to be happy for you. I want to celebrate with you when you take on the world, and I can't do that. I thought I could get my pilot's license or maybe go back to school, and everything would be fine, but you know what? All I've done is make myself miserable."

"This is it, isn't it?"

"I think so."

She stood, not wanting to cry. "Goodbye, Joe."

He stuck his hands in his pockets and walked her to the door. She wanted to touch him. One last kiss, one last embrace. But he had put up barriers that she couldn't break.

As he closed the door behind her, she heard him say, "I'll see you on *60 Minutes*."

AMANDA RETURNED to her old routine. She got up every morning at 4:30. When she couldn't sleep, she'd work on her computer at home. She was the pride and joy of Brown, Powers, and McGlynn. The Northcott case was winding down and another fat recovery was in the offing.

Now she didn't care.

Her nails were perfectly manicured—all ten of them. Her desk was spotless, perfectly organized. She found comfort in order.

Although there were things she allowed. She kept her apartment red. Someday she would change it, but for now Flambeau Red suited her.

She liked reading *Harry Potter*. She could hear Joe's voice reading to her. Sometimes it made her cry, but eventually the tears dried up.

NOVEMBER WENT BY in a haze. Joe still worked the extra hours. At first he had cut back, wanted to go back to his old ways, his old contentment, but after two weeks he realized that wasn't going to happen. Work made it easier to get through the days, but the nights were pretty much hell.

Late one night, he rounded the corner to his apartment building, and spotted Vincent and Bernie sitting on the stoop.

"Good evening, Joseph!" Vincent was wearing a purple smoking jacket and holding an unlit pipe in his hand.

"Nice duds."

Vincent beamed. "Why thank you, my good man."

"You're mighty peppy this evening," Joe said, fishing in his pocket for his keys.

"Got my first recovery check today. I've been thinking of moving. Perhaps a condo in Queens."

"I hear it's nice."

Bernie snorted. "Maybe, if you like those snobbish types."

Vincent twirled his pipe in the air. "I owe all this to Amanda, Joe. Where's she been? She's a real go-getter, your girl."

Joe wasn't going to answer that, so he forced a tired smile. "Yeah, she is."

TWO DAYS LATER he met Avery at his office before they went for dinner.

"Joe, you're turning into a recluse."

"Gee, I'll try harder."

"Now see, that's just what I mean. You have to get over her."

Joe shot him a look. "And you're the expert, right?"

"I've moved on."

Joe sometimes wondered. "Have you?"

"Of course I have, but twenty-year habits are difficult to break."

"Well, I'm going to move on, too. I'll find somebody new, settle down, maybe take up bowling."

Avery shook his head. "I must say that's the biggest pile of—" His cell phone rang and he pulled it out of his pocket. "Yes, Mother.

"Of course. I have it in my car.

"Well, I suppose so, but I'm going out with Joe.

"Yes, we're off to dine.

"Yes, yes, I understand. We'll be right there."

He put the phone back in his pocket. "She needs the new incense from the American Feng Shui Institute. Apparently it's quite hard to come by."

Joe was thrilled. "I have to come in with you?"

"She said she hasn't seen you in ages."

He looked straight ahead. Seeing Mom didn't make him nervous anymore. He'd been through worse and was still alive. Now he was just numb. "Let's go."

THE HOUSE was the same, his Mom was the same.

"Joseph Matthias Barrington!"

"Hi Mom." He hugged her, a little tighter than usual.

"How have you been? Come sit down."

She led the way to the living room. "You've lost weight? Something to drink?"

"No thanks."

He took stock of the room, it hadn't changed in the past ten years. Oh, maybe there were a few new pictures of Avery on the shrine. He walked over and started to count. Avery at graduation. Avery fishing on the coast. Avery...

And there were some new ones.

Of Joe.

Joe at Coney Island. Joe at the park. Joe in Amanda's living room. He was smiling, all happy. Love did that to you. It seemed like a lifetime ago, and it'd only been two months. Somewhere along the way he had lost his life and lost Amanda as well.

"Mom!"

"I'm right here, you don't have to shout."

He stared at himself at Coney Island. He'd been looking at her when the photographer shot the picture. It was frightening to see so much love in his eyes. "Where'd you get these?"

His mom moved next to him. "Can't you guess? From Amanda. Such a sweet girl."

Amanda must have emptied out her shelves after the big split. One final painful reminder that they had no future. "When did you see her last?"

"Oh, it's been ages now. She brought these over right after you two started seeing each other."

His mom had to be wrong. Amanda wouldn't have brought them over here. "Are you sure it wasn't more recent than that?"

"Well, of course I'm sure. I had to buy picture

hangers because we were all out, and then as I was getting ready to pay, I ran into Lorraine Ellsworth, and her daughter was with her. She looked ready to deliver that very day, she was so pregnant, and little Frank is...well, he must be about two months old by now. It was September, I'm certain."

He stared up at the wall. There he was. Right next to Avery. Never second place. Not with Amanda. "Are you sure?"

"Of course. I'm not that old, son."

His heart pumped with hope. Amanda had done that for him. He really had messed up. Maybe it wasn't too late.

"I love you, Mom." He hugged her and kissed her on the cheek.

"I love you, too, Joe." She followed him to the door. "Where are you going?"

"I'm going home, Mom."

"Well, good. Don't forget to eat something. You're looking much too thin."

AMANDA STARED at her computer, finishing up the last of the Northcott mediation. Another miraculous settlement. She looked up at the clock—10:00 p.m. She hated the nights alone worst of all. The intercom sounded insistently, as if someone was leaning on it.

Quickly, she went to the door and pressed the button, hoping no one was hurt.

"Amanda. Let me up."

The sound of his voice made her shake. "Joe?"

"Please."

She needed to be strong. "Why?"

"Amanda, we need to talk."

She leaned her head wearily against the door. "I don't think I want to see you."

"It's important." He sounded so urgent.

That just made her mad. "So important that's it's taken you two months to think of it?"

"No. Amanda?"

"Amanda?"

"What?"

"I've got to talk to you. I love you."

"That's not fair, Joe."

"Will you buzz me up? Please?"

She pressed the button, unlocked the door and then waited, absolutely refusing to get her hopes up.

He burst through the door.

"What's going on Joe? Why are you here?"

Joe motioned for her to sit down on the couch, his eyes animated. "To talk to you."

"Go ahead."

"I think we should try again."

Amanda couldn't control the wild jump in her heart. However, she was wiser now. "And with our successful track record, why do you think this time will be better?" She closed her eyes. Please, God.

"I finally figured it out."

That opened her eyes. "What?"

He started to pace around the room. All the restless energy was forcing him to move. "Amanda, when I grew up my parents measured a man by how much he made, how successful he was. A lot of people do that, me included. I figured you'd see me as second best and I couldn't understand how you, who have your life so together, could ever be happy with that. For you, I wanted to be first, I wanted to be *the best.*"

He knelt in front of her. "I owe you an apology. You're not like that."

Hope was a wondrous thing and she shook her head. "No. You could've just asked me that."

He took her hand. "I wouldn't have believed it."

"And you'd believe it now?" she asked carefully.

When he smiled up at her, she already knew the answer. For the first time in his life, Joe Barrington believed in himself.

"Yes. Amanda?"

The lump in her throat prevented speech. She nodded.

"Will you marry me? I can't live without you."

"You're sure about this?"

He looked so serious, so earnest, so in love. "Yeah."

It had been so long since she had touched him. She got down on the carpet next to him. "Good."

"It's not going to be easy, Amanda." He lowered his head.

"I know," she answered, scooting in closer.

"There'll have to be lots of compromises." He

kissed her neck. "And sacrifices." He moved her robe aside.

She buried her hands in his hair while his lips played on her skin. "And negotiations."

He eased her down to the carpet. "Second thing we do is paint all the walls."

"What's the first?"

His laugh was slow and smoky. "Let me show you."

_____Epilogue_____

IN EARLY SPRING, the flowers started blooming all over the city. In windowsills, in parks, outside stoops. For Amanda it was her favorite time of year. After all, she was going to be an April bride. She should have been looking over the latest malpractice claim that the firm had picked up, but instead she was thumbing through a bridal magazine.

Oh, well.

"Hey."

And there, in the doorway to her office—grinning rather foolishly—stood her fiancé.

Fiancé. She liked the way that sounded. "What are you doing here? You coming to take me back to Shakespeare's Garden?"

His eyes darkened, sending a sharp thrill down her spine. "Maybe later." Then he shook his head. "You're distracting me."

"From what?"

"We have to celebrate."

"Why?" Her mouth flew open. "You got your license, didn't you? You rat! Why didn't you say anything?"

He laughed, and it made her feel wonderful to

hear him like that. "No. I've got a few more hours in the air, and I swear, you'll be the first to know."

"Then what is it?"

"Well," he said, shutting the door behind him, quite firmly. There was such a brazen gleam in his eyes that she didn't even need to ask.

Oh, my.

"Joe, we shouldn't," she said with absolutely no enthusiasm.

"Amanda, we should," he replied, walking behind her desk.

She was easily convinced. "Well, maybe we should." She held up a hand. "Wait. First, what are we celebrating?"

He kissed her neck, his afternoon stubble rough and decadent, and then he pressed his mouth against her ear, whispering softly in a way that never failed to thrill her. "*60 Minutes* called."

More fabulous reading from
the Queen of Sizzle!

LORI
FOSTER

with

*Forever
and Always*

Back by popular demand are the scintillating stories of
Gabe and Jordan Buckhorn. They're gorgeous, sexy
and single...at least for now!

Available wherever books are sold—September 2002.

And look for Lori's *brand-new* single title,
CASEY in early 2003

If you enjoyed what you just read,
then we've got an offer you can't resist!

Take 2 bestselling
love stories FREE!
Plus get a FREE surprise gift!